D0410671

Theodore Boone
THE ACCUSED

Also by John Grisham

A Time to Kill
The Firm
The Pelican Brief
The Client
The Chamber
The Rainmaker
The Runaway Jury
The Partner
The Street Lawyer
The Testament
The Brethren
A Painted House
Skipping Christmas
The Summons
The King of Torts
Bleachers
The Last Juror
The Broker
Playing for Pizza
The Appeal
The Associate
Ford County
The Confession
The Litigators
Calico Joe

Theodore Boone
Theodore Boone: The Abduction

Non-fiction
The Innocent Man

John
Grisham

Theodore Boone
THE ACCUSED

HODDER &
STOUGHTON

First published in Great Britain in 2012 by Hodder & Stoughton
An Hachette UK company

1

Copyright © Belfry Holdings, Inc. 2012

A CIP catalogue record for this title is available from the British Library.

Hardback ISBN 978 1 444 72888 0
Trade Paperback ISBN 978 1 444 72889 7

Printed and bound by Clays Ltd, St Ives plc

Hodder & Stoughton policy is to use papers that are natural, renewable and recy-
clable products and made from wood grown in sustainable
forests. The logging and manufacturing processes are expected to
conform to the environmental regulations of the country of origin.

Hodder & Stoughton Ltd
338 Euston Road
London NW1 3BH

www.hodder.co.uk

Theodore Boone
THE ACCUSED

Chapter I

The accused was a wealthy man by the name of Pete Duffy, and his alleged crime was murder. According to the police and the prosecutors, Mr. Duffy strangled his lovely wife in their attractive home on the sixth fairway of a golf course where he, the accused, was playing golf that day, alone. If convicted, he would spend the rest of his life in prison. If acquitted, he would walk out of the courtroom a free man. As things turned out, the jury did not find him guilty, or not guilty.

This was his second trial. Four months earlier, the first trial had ended suddenly when Judge Henry Gantry decided it would be unfair to continue. He declared a mistrial and sent everyone home, including Pete Duffy, who remained free on bond. In most murder cases, the accused cannot afford to post a bond and stay out of jail while waiting on a trial. But because Mr. Duffy had money and good lawyers, he had been free as a bird since the police found his wife's body and the State accused him of killing her. He had been seen around town—dining in his favorite restaurants, watching basketball games at Stratten College, attending church (with greater frequency), and, of course, playing lots of golf. As he waited on his first trial, he seemed unconcerned with the prospect of a trial and the possibility of prison. Now, though, facing his second trial, and with a new eyewitness ready to be used by the prosecution, Pete Duffy was rumored to be very worried.

The new eyewitness was Bobby Escobar, a nineteen-year-old illegal immigrant who was working at the golf course on the day Mrs. Duffy was murdered. He saw Mr. Duffy enter his home at about the same time she died, then hurry away and resume his golf game. For a lot of reasons, Bobby did not come forward until the first trial was underway. Once Judge Gantry heard Bobby's story, he declared a mistrial. Now, with Bobby ready to testify, most of the folks in Strattenburg, who had been closely watching the Duffy case, were expecting a guilty verdict. It was almost impossible to find someone who believed Pete Duffy did not kill his wife.

And it was also difficult to find a person who did not

want to watch the trial. A murder trial in the Strattenburg Courthouse was a rare event—indeed, murder was rare in Stratten County—and a large crowd began gathering at 8:00 a.m., just after the front doors of the courthouse opened. The jury had been selected three days earlier. It was time for the courtroom drama to begin.

At 8:40, Mr. Mount got his eighth-grade class quiet and called the roll. All sixteen boys were present. Homeroom lasted for only ten minutes before the boys went off to first period Spanish with Madame Monique.

Mr. Mount was in a hurry. He said, "Okay, men, you know that today is the first day of the Pete Duffy trial, round two. We were allowed to watch the first day of the first trial, but, as you know, my request to watch the second trial was denied."

Several of the boys hissed and booed.

Mr. Mount raised his hands. "Enough. However, our esteemed principal, Mrs. Gladwell, has agreed to allow Theo to watch the opening of the trial and report back to us. Theo."

Theodore Boone jumped to his feet, and, like the lawyers he watched and admired, walked purposefully to the front of the room. He carried a yellow legal pad, just like a real lawyer. He stood by Mr. Mount's desk, paused for a second, and looked at the class as if he were indeed a trial lawyer preparing to address the jury.

Since both of his parents were lawyers, and he had practically been raised in their law offices, and he hung out in courtrooms while the other eighth graders at Strattenburg Middle School were playing sports and taking guitar lessons and doing all the things that normal thirteen-year-olds tend to do, and since he loved the law and studied it and watched it and talked about little else, the rest of his class was quick to yield to Theo when discussing legal matters. When it came to the law, Theo had no competition, at least not in Mr. Mount's eighth-grade homeroom.

Theo began, "Well, we saw the first day of the first trial four months ago, so you know the lineups and the players. The lawyers are the same. The charges are the same. Mr. Duffy is still Mr. Duffy. There is a different jury this time around, and, of course, there is the issue of a new eyewitness who did not testify during the first trial."

"Guilty!" yelled Woody from the back of the room. Several others chimed in and added their agreement.

"All right," Theo said. "Show of hands. Who thinks Pete Duffy is guilty?"

Fourteen of sixteen hands shot upward with no hesitation whatsoever. Chase Whipple, a mad scientist who took pride in never agreeing with the majority, sat with his arms folded across his chest.

Theo did not vote, but instead became irritated. "This is ridiculous! How can you vote guilty before the trial has started, before we know what the witnesses will say, before anything happens? We've talked about the presumption of innocence. In our system, a person charged with a crime is presumed to be innocent until proven guilty. Pete Duffy will walk into the courtroom this morning completely innocent, and will remain innocent until all the witnesses have testified and all the proof is before the jury. The presumption of innocence, remember?"

Mr. Mount stood in a corner and watched Theo at his best. He had seen this before, many times. The kid was a natural on his feet, the star of the Eighth-Grade Debate Team, of which Mr. Mount was the faculty adviser.

Theo pressed on, still pretending to be indignant at his classmates' rush to judgment. "And proof beyond a reasonable doubt, remember? What's the matter with you guys?"

"Guilty!" Woody yelled again, and got some laughs.

Theo knew it was a lost cause. He said, "Okay, okay, can I go now?"

"Sure," Mr. Mount replied. The bell rang loudly and

all sixteen boys headed for the door. Theo darted into the hallway and raced to the front office where Miss Gloria, the school's secretary, was on the phone. She liked Theo because his mother had handled her first divorce, and because Theo had once given her some unofficial advice when her brother was caught driving drunk. She handed Theo a yellow release form, signed by Mrs. Gladwell, and he was off. The clock above her desk gave the time as exactly 8:47.

Outside, at the bike rack by the flagpole, Theo unlocked his chain, wrapped it around the handlebars, and sped away. If he obeyed the rules of the road and stayed on the streets, he would arrive in front of the courthouse in fifteen minutes. But, if he took the usual shortcuts, and raced through an alley or two, and cut across a backyard here and another one there, and ran at least two STOP signs, Theo could make it in about ten minutes. On this day, he did not have time to spare. He knew the courtroom was already packed. He would be lucky to get a seat.

He flew through an alley, got airborne twice, then darted through the backyard of a man he knew, an unpleasant man, a man who wore a uniform and tried to act as though he were a real officer of the law when in fact he was little more than a part-time security guard. His name was Buck Boland, (or Buck Baloney, as some people whispered behind his back), and Theo saw him occasionally hanging around the courthouse. As Theo flew across Mr. Boland's backyard, he heard a loud, angry voice. "Get outta here, kid!" Theo turned to his left just in time to see Mr. Boland throw a rock in his direction. The rock landed very close by, and Theo pedaled even harder.

That was close, he thought. Perhaps he should find another route.

Nine minutes after leaving the school, Theo wheeled to a stop in front of the Stratten County Courthouse, quickly chained his bike to the rack, and sprinted inside, up the grand staircase and to the massive front doors of Judge Gantry's courtroom. There was a crowd at the door—spectators in a line trying to get in, and TV cameras with their bright lights, and several grim-faced deputies trying to keep order. Theo's least favorite deputy in all of Strattenburg was an old grouchy man named Gossett, and, as luck would have it, Gossett saw Theo trying to ease his way through the crowd.

"Where do you think you're going, Theo?" Gossett growled.

It should be obvious where I'm going, Theo thought quickly to himself. Where else would I be going at this moment, at the beginning of the biggest murder trial in the history of our county? But being a wise guy would not help matters.

Theo whipped out his release from school and said,

sweetly, "I have permission from my principal to watch the trial, sir." Gossett snatched the release and glared at it as if he might have to shoot Theo if his paperwork didn't measure up. Theo thought about saying, "If you need some help, I'll read it for you," but, again, bit his tongue.

Gossett said, "This is from school. This is not a pass to get inside. Do you have permission from Judge Gantry?"

"Yes, sir," Theo said.

"Let me see it."

"It's not in writing. Judge Gantry gave me verbal permission to watch the trial."

Gossett frowned even harder, shook his head with great authority, and said, "Sorry, Theo. The courtroom is packed. There are no more seats. We're turning people away."

Theo took his release and tried to appear as if he might burst into tears. He backtracked, turned around, and headed down the long hallway. When Gossett could no longer see him, he ducked through a narrow door and bounced down a utility staircase, one used only by the janitors and service technicians. On the first floor, he eased along a dark, cramped corridor that ran under the main courtroom above, then stepped nonchalantly into a break room where the courthouse employees gathered for coffee, doughnuts, and gossip.

"Well, hello, Theo," said lovely Jenny, by far Theo's favorite clerk in the entire courthouse.

"Hello, Jenny," he said with a smile as he kept walking across the small room. He disappeared into a utility closet, came out the other side onto a landing which led to another hidden staircase. In decades past, this had been used to haul convicts from the jail to the main courtroom to face the wrath of the judges, but now it was seldom used. The old courthouse was a maze of cramped passageways and narrow staircases, and Theo knew every one of them.

He entered the courtroom from a side door next to the jury box. The place was buzzing with the nervous chatter of spectators about to see something dramatic. Uniformed guards milled about, chatting with one another and looking important. There was a crowd at the main door as people were still trying to get in. On the left side of the courtroom, in the third row behind the defense table, Theo saw a familiar face.

It was his uncle, Ike, and he was saving a seat for his favorite (and only) nephew. Theo wiggled and darted down the row and wedged himself into a tight spot next to Ike.

Chapter 2

Ike Boone had once been a lawyer. In fact, he had once been in the same offices as Theo's parents. The three Boones had survived a rocky partnership until Ike ran afoul of the law and got himself into trouble, big trouble. So much trouble that the State Bar Association revoked his license to practice law. Now, he worked as an accountant and tax adviser to several small businesses in Strattenburg. He had no family to speak of and was generally an unhappy old man. He liked to think of himself as a loner, a misfit, a rebel who dressed like an old hippie and wore his long, white hair pulled back into a ponytail. On this day he was wearing typical Ike attire—ancient sandals with no socks, faded jeans, a red T-shirt under a checkered sports coat with frayed sleeves.

"Thanks, Ike," Theo whispered as he settled into his place.

Ike smiled and said nothing. He was to Theo's right. To Theo's left was an attractive middle-aged woman he had never seen. As Theo looked around, he noticed several lawyers seated among the spectators. His own parents claimed to be far too busy to waste time watching the trial, though Theo knew they were keenly interested in it. His mother was a well-respected divorce lawyer with lots of clients, and his father handled real estate transactions and never went to court. Theo would one day be a great courtroom lawyer, one who stayed away from divorce and real estate. Or, he might be a great judge like his pal Henry Gantry. He couldn't decide, but he had plenty of time. He was only thirteen.

The jury box was empty, and because Theo had watched so many trials he knew that the jurors were not brought into the courtroom until everyone else was settled. There was a large square clock on the wall far above the judge's bench, and at 8:59, the prosecutors appeared from a side door with their usual air of great importance. They were led by Jack Hogan, a veteran who had been hounding criminals in Strattenburg for many years. In the first trial four months earlier, Theo had been greatly impressed with Mr. Hogan's courtroom skills, and for weeks afterward

Theo had considered becoming a prosecutor, the man the entire town would turn to when a horrible crime had been committed. Mr. Hogan was surrounded by several of his younger prosecutors and investigators. They made quite a team.

Across the aisle, the defense table was deserted—not a single member of the Pete Duffy trial team was present. Just behind it, though, in the first row, Theo could see Omar Cheepe and his sidekick, Paco, a couple of thugs hired by the defense to investigate things and cause trouble. As the clock ticked and the crowd settled in, it seemed odd, at least to Theo, that only half the lawyers were present and ready to go. Judge Gantry believed in being prompt, and when nothing happened at 9:00 a.m. sharp, the crowd stared at the clock—9:05, then 9:10. Finally, at 9:15, the defense team entered the courtroom and took seats. It was led by Clifford Nance, a well-known trial lawyer, who, at that moment, looked pale and perplexed. He leaned over the bar and huddled with Omar Cheepe and Paco, and it was apparent that something was wrong.

There was no sign of Pete Duffy, who should have been sitting at the defense table next to Clifford Nance.

Omar Cheepe and Paco suddenly left the courtroom.

At 9:20, a bailiff stood and yelled, "All rise for the

Court." As he did so, Judge Henry Gantry entered from behind his bench, his black robe flowing after him. The bailiff went on, "Hear ye, hear ye, the Criminal Court of the Tenth District is now in session, The Honorable Henry Gantry presiding. Let all who have matters come forth. May God bless this court."

"Please be seated," Judge Gantry said, and the crowd, still in the process of rising, suddenly fell back again.

Judge Gantry glared at Clifford Nance and took a deep breath. All eyes followed his, and Mr. Nance looked even paler. Finally, Judge Gantry said, "Mr. Nance, where is the defendant, Peter Duffy?"

Clifford Nance slowly got to his feet. He cleared his throat, and when he finally spoke his rich voice sounded scratchy and defeated. "Your Honor, I do not know. Mr. Duffy was scheduled to be in my office this morning at 7:00 a.m. for a pretrial meeting, but he did not show. He has not called, faxed, e-mailed, or texted me or anyone on my staff. We have called his phone numbers many times but got nothing. We've gone to his home, but no one is there. We are, at this moment, searching for him, but it appears as though he has vanished."

Theo listened in disbelief, as did everyone in the courtroom. A deputy stood and said, "Your Honor, if I may?"

"Proceed," said Judge Gantry.

"This is the first we've heard of this. Had we been notified earlier, we could have begun a search."

"Well, start looking now," Judge Gantry said angrily. He was obviously upset at the absence of Pete Duffy. He rapped his gavel and said, "We'll be in recess for an hour. Please tell the jurors to make themselves comfortable back there." And with that, Judge Gantry disappeared through a door behind his bench.

For a moment or two the spectators sat in stunned disbelief, as if they might see Pete Duffy walk in any moment now if they simply kept waiting. Then there were whispers and light chatter, then movements as several stood and began milling about. No one left, though, because no one wanted to take the chance of losing a seat. Surely, Pete Duffy would arrive any minute, apologize for being late, blame it on a flat tire or something, and the trial would go on.

Ten minutes passed. Theo watched the lawyers slowly ease toward the center of the courtroom and engage in hushed conversations. Jack Hogan and Clifford Nance huddled as if to compare notes, both men frowning gravely.

"What do you think, Ike?" Theo asked softly.

"Looks like he skipped out."

"What does this mean?"

"It means a lot of things. Duffy put up some real estate to secure his bond, to guarantee his appearance in court, so that property will be forfeited and he'll lose it. Of course, if he has indeed skipped out, he's not too worried about property here because he'll spend the rest of his life on the run. He'll be a fugitive, until they catch him."

"Will they catch him?"

"They usually do. His face will be everywhere—all over the Internet, on Wanted posters in the post office and every police station in the country. It will be difficult to avoid capture, but there have been some famous cases of fugitives who are never caught. They usually get out of the country and go to South America or some place. I'm surprised. I didn't think Pete Duffy had the guts to make a run for it."

"Guts?"

"Sure. Think about it, Theo. The guy killed his wife and got lucky when the first trial ended in a mistrial. He knew that would not happen again, so he was looking at a lifetime in prison. Me, I'd rather take my chances on the run. He's probably buried some money somewhere. Got himself some new papers, a new name, maybe a pal who's helping. Knowing Duffy, he's probably got some young woman hooked into his scheme. Pretty smart move if you ask me."

Ike made it sound like a real adventure, but Theo wasn't

so sure. As the clock approached 10:00 a.m., he gazed at the empty chair where the defendant was supposed to be and found it impossible to believe that Pete Duffy had jumped bond, skipped town, and was now prepared to live the life of a fugitive.

Omar Cheepe and Paco reappeared and huddled with Clifford Nance. From the way they shook their heads, whispered urgently, and exchanged hard looks, it was obvious the situation had not improved. Pete Duffy was nowhere to be found.

A bailiff rounded up the lawyers and herded them into Judge Gantry's chambers for another meeting. Several deputies were telling jokes near the jury box. The noise level was rising as the crowd grew restless and frustrated.

"I'm getting kind of bored, Theo," Ike said. A few others had left the courtroom.

"I might hang around," Theo said. His only other option was to return to school, empty-handed, and suffer through classes. The release from the principal plainly stated that Theo was excused from school until 1:00 p.m., and he did not want to return any sooner, trial or no trial.

"Are you stopping by this afternoon?" Ike asked. It was a Monday, and the Boone family rituals required Theo to stop by Ike's office every Monday afternoon for a visit.

"Sure," Theo said.

Ike smiled and said, "See you then."

After he was gone, Theo weighed the pros and cons of the situation. He was disappointed that the biggest criminal trial in the recent history of Strattenburg had evidently been sidetracked, and that he would not get the chance to watch Jack Hogan and Clifford Nance go toe-to-toe like two gladiators. But, he was also relieved that Bobby Escobar would not be forced to testify and point the finger of guilt at Pete Duffy. Theo had played a big role in bringing Bobby to the attention of Judge Gantry during the first trial, and Theo knew that Duffy's lawyers and his thugs, especially Omar Cheepe and Paco, were keeping an eye on him. Theo preferred not to have the attention.

In fact, as the clock ticked and the crowd waited, Theo decided that the sudden disappearance of Pete Duffy was a good thing, at least for him. Selfishly, he was pleased.

Two men behind Theo were having a disagreement. In low voices, they were arguing over the fact that Duffy had been allowed to post a bond. The first man said: "I'll bet Gantry takes some heat for this. If he had denied bail, Duffy would have been locked up while he waited for his trial, the same as every other defendant charged with murder. No one gets bail in a murder case. Gantry caved in because Duffy has money."

The second man said: "I doubt it. Why not allow a

defendant to post bail and get out? He's innocent until proven guilty, right? Why lock up a guy before he's convicted? Murder or otherwise? You can't punish a guy just because he has money. Duffy's bail was a million dollars. He put up some property and nobody complained, until now, anyway."

Theo tended to side with the second guy. The first one responded: "Until now? That's the whole point. Bail is supposed to secure his appearance in court. Guess what? He's not here. AWOL, flew the coop, over the wall, we'll never see him again because Gantry granted bail."

"They'll find him."

"I'll bet they don't. He's probably in Mexico City right now, getting his face worked on by some plastic surgeons who got rich re-doing the eyes and noses of drug lords. I'll bet they never find Pete Duffy."

"I'll bet you twenty bucks he's back here in thirty days, in jail."

"You got it, twenty bucks."

There was a rustle of activity and the bailiffs sprang to attention. The lawyers streamed out of Judge Gantry's chambers and took their places. The spectators scurried for their seats and became silent. "Remain seated," a bailiff barked. Judge Gantry assumed his position on the bench. He rapped his gavel loudly and said, "Order. Bring in the jury, please."

It was 11:00 a.m. The jurors filed into the courtroom and took their seats in the jury box. When they were in place, Judge Gantry looked sternly at Clifford Nance and said, "Mr. Nance, where is the defendant?"

Nance rose slowly and replied, "Your Honor, I do not know. We have had no contact with Mr. Duffy since ten thirty last night."

Judge Gantry looked at Jack Hogan and said, "Mr. Hogan."

"Your Honor, we have no choice but to move for a mistrial."

"And I have no choice but to grant one." Judge Gantry then turned and addressed the jury. "Ladies and gentlemen, it appears as though the defendant, Mr. Peter Duffy, has disappeared. He has been free on bond, awaiting this trial, and, well, he has evidently vanished. The sheriff's department is conducting a search and the FBI has been notified. Without a defendant, we cannot proceed at this time. I apologize for the inconvenience, and, once again, I thank you for your willingness to serve. You are dismissed."

One of the jurors slowly raised her hand and asked, "But, Judge, what if they find him this afternoon, or tomorrow?"

Judge Gantry seemed surprised by a question coming from the jury box. "Well, I suppose it depends on how he is found. Let's say they catch him at a border, trying to sneak out of the country, then he'll be brought back here to face additional charges. That would certainly affect his strategy at trial, so he would be entitled to a delay. But let's suppose he's found somewhere around here and has a valid excuse for not showing up this morning. In that case, I would revoke his bond, or bail, put him in jail, and reschedule the trial as soon as possible."

This satisfied the juror and Theo as well.

"Court is adjourned," Judge Gantry said, and pecked his gavel once again.

Theo waited and waited, and finally left when a bailiff was turning off the lights. He had no place to go but school, and he biked in that general direction. Two blocks away from the courthouse, a black Jeep Cherokee eased alongside Theo. Its passenger window came down, and Paco's swarthy head leaned out. He smiled but said nothing.

Theo braked and they passed. Why would they be following him?

He was rattled and made the quick decision to duck through an alley and cross a backyard. He was half looking over his shoulder when a large man stepped in front of him and grabbed the handlebars of his bike. "Hey, kid!" he growled, now face-to-face with Theo.

It was Buck Baloney, breathing fire and ready for war.

"Stay outta my yard, okay?" he growled, still gripping the handlebars.

"Okay, okay, sorry," Theo said, afraid of getting slapped.

"What's your name?" Buck hissed.

"Theodore Boone. Let go of my bike."

Buck was dressed in an ill-fitting and cheap uniform with the words ALL-PRO SECURITY stitched on the sleeves. And, he had a rather large pistol on his belt.

"Stop cutting across my yard, you understand?"

"I got it," Theo said.

Buck let go, and Theo sped away without getting shot. Suddenly, he was excited about returning to school, and to the safety of his classroom.

Chapter 3

Theo checked in at the front office and returned his release form. His classmates were in fourth period Chemistry, and Theo wanted to avoid walking in late. Instead, he went to Mr. Mount's tiny office, down the hall from his classroom. The door was open, and, luckily, Mr. Mount was at his desk, eating a sandwich and watching the local news on his laptop.

"Have a seat," Mr. Mount said, and Theo sat in the only other chair in the office.

"So I guess you know," Theo said.

"Oh, yes. It's all over the news." Mr. Mount slid his laptop over a few inches so Theo could have a better look. The sheriff was talking to a gang of reporters. He was saying that there was no sign of Mr. Duffy. They had searched his home and found nothing. Both of his vehicles, a Mercedes sedan and a Ford SUV, were locked and parked in the garage. Evidently Mr. Duffy had played golf, alone, late Sunday afternoon and was seen leaving the course by a caddy. He was in his golf cart and headed in the general direction of his home on the sixth fairway, the same route the caddy had seen him take many times after playing a round. At 10:30 on Sunday night, Pete Duffy spoke by phone to Clifford Nance, and, according to Nance, agreed to meet with his defense team at 7:00 a.m. sharp for a lengthy prep session.

Pete Duffy lived two miles east of town in a fairly new development called Waverly Creek, an upscale residential community designed around three golf courses and meant to offer its residents a lot of privacy. Entry and exit were monitored twenty-four hours a day by guards at gates, with surveillance cameras recording everything. The sheriff was positive Pete Duffy had not left Waverly Creek during the night through one of the gates. "There are some gravel roads leading in and out, and I suppose that's where he went," the sheriff speculated. It was obvious the sheriff had little patience with reporters.

He went on to say there was no indication, yet, of how Pete Duffy fled. On foot, bike, scooter, four-wheeler, golf cart—they had not been able to determine that. But, there was no record of Duffy owning a scooter, motorcycle, or other type of vehicle that required registration.

In response to random and thoughtless questions, the sheriff explained that (1) there was no evidence of an accomplice involved in the Duffy escape; (2) there was no suicide note, in the event he jumped from a bridge or some other dramatic stunt; (3) there was no evidence of foul play, as if an intruder, for some unknown reason, wanted to eliminate Duffy the night before he was to stand trial; and (4) so far, they had found no witness who laid eyes on Duffy after the caddy saw him drive away with his golf clubs.

The sheriff finally had enough and excused himself. The news station switched back to the studio, where a couple of anchors launched into a windy summary of what little had just been said by the sheriff.

"So where is he?" Mr. Mount asked, chewing on his sandwich.

"I can't believe he would take off in the middle of the night on foot and through the woods," Theo said. "What's your theory?"

"An accomplice. Duffy is not the outdoor type, not a man who understands the woods and what it takes to survive. I'll bet he slipped away from his house, after midnight when his neighbors were sound asleep, used a bicycle because he didn't want to make noise, and rode a mile or two down a trail where his accomplice was waiting. They tossed the bike in the trunk of the car, or the back of a pickup, and away they went. He wasn't due in court until 9:00 a.m., so they had a head start of seven or eight hours."

"You're really into this, aren't you?" Theo asked, amused.

"Sure. And you're not?"

"Of course, but I haven't given it as much thought as you. Where is he right now?"

"Far away. The cops have no idea what kind of vehicle they're driving, so they're home free until more clues pop up. He could be anywhere."

"You think they'll catch him?"

"Something tells me they will not. This might be the perfect escape, especially if he has an accomplice."

Mr. Mount was in his midthirties and, at least in Theo's opinion, was by far the coolest teacher at the school. His father was a judge and his older brother was a lawyer, and he often talked of leaving the classroom and going to law school. He sponsored the Eighth-Grade Debate Team. Theo was his star, and so the two had developed a close friendship. As they watched the news on the laptop, both minds were spinning wild scenarios about what had happened to Pete Duffy. How had he really managed to disappear?

"I guess we'll discuss this in Government tomorrow," Theo said.

"Are you kidding? This town will talk of nothing else for the next two days."

The bell rang and Theo was suddenly ready to leave. Lunch was only a twenty-minute break and there was no time to waste. The halls were instantly crowded as five sections of eighth graders hurried from their classrooms, to their lockers, and to the cafeteria.

The Strattenburg Middle School had been modernized a few years earlier, and one of the more popular improvements was the new lockers. They were wide and deep, and made of wood instead of the old noisy metal boxes that had lined the halls for decades. Keys were not needed because each locker had an entry panel similar to the keypad of a phone. Punch in your five- or six-digit secret code, and the door clicked open.

Theo's pass code was Judge (58343), in honor of his beloved dog. He pulled open the door, and immediately knew something was wrong. Several things were missing. Theo occasionally suffered asthma attacks, which required him to use an inhaler. He kept one in his pocket at all times, and he kept a three-pack of reserves in his locker. These were gone, as was a blue and red Minnesota Twins cap he kept on a hook in case it rained. Two unused notepads were missing. His books were there, stacked on top of each other.

He froze for a moment, staring into the locker to make sure he wasn't dreaming, then glanced around to see if anyone (the thief?) might be watching. No one seemed to be paying attention to him. He shifted his books, poked around, and finally came to the conclusion that his locker had been broken into. He had been robbed!

Small-time thievery happened occasionally. The new lockers, though, with their advanced security system, had virtually eliminated such break-ins. He looked down the hall and up to a spot above a large wall clock. There was an empty bracket where a security camera had once been installed. The camera was gone because the school was in the process of updating its video-monitoring system.

Theo wasn't sure what to do. If he reported the theft, he would spend the next hour or so in the principal's office filling out paperwork. And, worse still, he would have to deal with a hundred nosy questions from his friends and classmates. As he walked to the cafeteria, he decided to wait, to think about it, to try and figure out how someone could learn his code and break in his locker. He could always report it tomorrow.

He paid two dollars for a bowl of spaghetti, a piece of cold bread, and a bottle of water. He sat with Chase and Woody, and the conversation quickly turned to the Duffy trial and disappearance. As they talked, Theo could not help but survey the cafeteria. It was filled with eighth graders, none of whom was wearing his Twins cap. As far as Theo knew, he was the only Twins fan in Strattenburg.

During Mr. Mount's study hall that afternoon, Theo gave a quick description of what he'd seen in court that morning, then they watched the local news as the Duffy story continued to dominate every conversation in town. Still no sign of the fugitive. An FBI agent was interviewed and asked the community for leads. So far, they had no clues into his disappearance. Much was being made of the one million dollar bond he had posted to remain free on bail, and this led to several stories about his financial situation. A former business partner claimed to know Duffy well, and offered the opinion that he ". . . always kept a lot of cash . . ." stashed away in secret places. This juicy bit of gossip sent the local reporters into a frenzy.

After school, Theo checked his locker again, and things appeared to be fine. Nothing else had been taken. He thought about changing his pass code, but decided to wait. Changing the code was no simple matter because all codes were registered with the principal's office. The school maintained the right to open any locker at any time, for good cause, but this was seldom done. On at least one prior occasion, Theo had failed to properly close his locker, and the following day was puzzled to find its door shut, but unlocked. This was not uncommon in the seventh and eighth grades because the closing mechanism required a student to press and hold the CLOSE button for a full three seconds. Twelve- and thirteen-year-olds can get in a hurry, or get distracted, and fail to hold the button long enough.

By the time Theo left the building and walked to his bike, he had convinced himself that his locker had been vandalized, but not broken into. He vowed to be more vigilant.

Theo soon had another problem. He unchained his bike, wrapped the chain around his handlebars as always, and pushed off. Instantly, he realized his front tire was flat. He got off his bike, examined the tire, and found a small gash where someone had punctured the sidewall.

Theo was in the midst of an unlucky run with his bike tires. In the previous three months, he had collected two nails, a piece of glass from a soft drink bottle, a jagged piece of metal, and he had punctured two front tires on account of reckless riding. His father was not happy with this and when the subject of the cost of bike tires came up over dinner, things were tense.

This latest puncture, though, was no accident. Someone had deliberately stuck a sharp object into his tire.

He waited until his friends rode away, then began the

humiliating journey downtown, pushing his bike along streets that now seemed much longer, wondering who would do such a thing to him, and trying to put this latest act of vandalism in the context of a day that had not gone well. The excitement of the trial had vanished; Omar Cheepe and Paco had followed him as he rode to school; Buck Baloney had almost hit him with a rock and then caught him the second time he dashed through his backyard; someone had vandalized his locker; and now this—a slashed bike tire that would cut deeply into his savings account.

Theo couldn't help but take an occasional glance over his shoulder, certain that eyes were watching.

Gil's bike shop was downtown, three blocks from the courthouse, on a narrow street lined with small mom-and-pop stores. There was a cleaners, a shoe shop, photo lab, bakery, a knife sharpener that owed Ike money for tax services, and a couple of delis. Theo took pride in knowing every owner. Gil was one of his favorites—a short, round man with an awesome belly that was always partially hidden by a thick work apron covered in dirt and grime. Gil sold bikes and he loved to repair them. His shop was jam-packed with models of every size and color, with the smaller ones hanging from large hooks in the ceiling and the fancier mountain bikes lined up in the front windows.

Theo rolled his through the front door, thoroughly

defeated by the day. Gil was sitting on a stool by the back counter, drinking coffee. "Well, well," he said. "Look who's back."

"Hey, Gil," Theo said. "Another flat tire."

"What happened?" Gil asked as he rolled himself off the stool and waddled over.

"Looks like sabotage."

Gil lifted the handlebars, spun the front tire until he found the hole in it, and exhaled a soft whistle. "You make somebody mad?"

"Not that I know of."

"Small penknife, I'd say. Certainly no accident. Can't do anything with it. Theo, you gotta have a new one."

"I was afraid of that. How much?"

"You should know the price better than me. Eighteen bucks. You want me to send the bill to your dad?"

"No, he's fed up with me and my bike tires. I'll pay for this one, but I can't swing eighteen dollars today."

"How much can you pay now?"

"I can give you ten tomorrow, and the rest in a couple of weeks. You have my word, Gil. I'll even sign a promissory note."

"I thought you were a lawyer, Theo."

"Sort of."

"Well, then, you need to do some more research. A

person has to be eighteen years old before he can enter into a valid contract, including a promissory note."

"Sure, sure, I know that."

"Let's just do an old-fashioned handshake deal. Ten bucks tomorrow, and the other eight bucks in two weeks." Gil extended his dirty and chubby right hand, and Theo shook it.

Fifteen minutes later he was flying down Park Street, happy to be so mobile again, but still wondering if the day could get any worse. He was also debating about how much of his bad luck should be reported to his parents. The farther he got away from his vandalized locker, the less important it seemed. Theo could live with those losses, irritating as they were. The slashed tire was another story because it involved a weapon.

As he approached the law offices of Boone & Boone, Theo suddenly had a frightening thought. What if the same person had robbed his locker, then slashed his tire as well?

Chapter 4

Boone & Boone was a small law firm on a street full of other lawyers, accountants, and architects. All of the buildings along that section of Park Street had once been homes, long before Theo was born.

He carried his bike up the front steps and leaned it against the wall, near the door, its customary parking place. He glanced around, just to make sure no one was watching him, or his bike. Inside the front door, the reception area was the turf of Elsa Miller, the firm's head secretary and sometimes its boss. She was a spry, hyperactive woman who was old enough to be Theo's grandmother, and she often acted as though she was.

As always, she bounced from her chair behind her

desk and assaulted Theo the moment she saw him. There was a fierce hug, a painful yank of the earlobe, a tussling of his hair, but, thankfully, no kissing. Elsa understood that thirteen-year-old boys did not want to be kissed by anyone. During this attack, and Theo considered it nothing less, she was talking nonstop. "Theo! How was your day? Are you hungry? Does that shirt match those pants? Have you finished your homework? Have you heard the news about Pete Duffy jumping off a bridge?"

"Jumping off a bridge?" Theo repeated, taking a step back and freeing himself from her embrace.

"Well, that's just one theory, but, good gosh, there is so much gossip racing around this town right now."

"I was in court this morning when he didn't show," Theo said proudly.

"You were?!"

"Yes."

Elsa retreated as quickly as she had attacked, allowing Judge to come forth and say hello. Judge spent his days easing around the office, checking on everyone, sleeping in various places, and always looking for something to eat. He usually waited for Theo in one of two places—either Theo's chair back in his office, or on a small bed at Elsa's feet, supposedly providing protection for the firm but doing nothing of the sort.

"There are pecan brownies in the kitchen," Elsa said.

"Who made them?" Theo asked. It was a fair question. Elsa's pecan brownies were somewhat edible, if one were starving, but the wedges occasionally brought in by Dorothy, the real estate secretary, were not. They looked like brick mortar and tasted like mud, and not even Judge would give them a sniff.

"I made them, Theo, and they're delicious."

"Yours are perfect," Theo said as he headed down the hall.

"Your mother is in court and your father is across town wrapping up a real estate deal," Elsa said. An important part of her job was to keep track of everybody, especially Mr. and Mrs. Boone, and this was easy because she was in charge of their schedules. But Elsa, at any given moment, could give you the precise whereabouts of Dorothy, and of Vince, the paralegal who worked under Mrs. Boone. Add Judge and Theo to the list, and Elsa knew everyone's appointments, lunch dates, coffee dates, doctors' visits, depositions, loan closings, birthdays, vacations, anniversaries, even funerals. She once gave Dorothy a sympathy card after her father's funeral—three years to the day after the old guy was buried.

According to the Boone master plan for daily living, Theo was expected to (1) arrive at the office each day after school, where he (2) checked in with Elsa and suffered through her rituals, then (3) stopped by his mother's office for a quick hello, then (4) walked upstairs, with Judge close at his heels, where he gave his father a rundown of the day's activities, then, (5) after a quick word with Dorothy, and (6) another one with Vince, he (7) went to his small office in the back of the building and cranked out his homework, which was to be done before dinner. Of course, if he had something else to do, like work on a merit badge or watch his classmates play soccer or basketball, he was excused from the office ritual. He was a kid, an only child, and his parents, strict as they were, understood the realities of raising a well-rounded thirteen-year-old.

Theo closed the door to his tiny office and pulled his laptop from his backpack. He checked the local news for an update on the search for Pete Duffy. There was not a single word about the man jumping off a bridge, and this did not surprise Theo. Elsa was known to exaggerate.

Theo found it difficult to concentrate, but after two hours the homework was complete, for the most part. Elsa was tidying up her desk and preparing to leave. Both Mr. and Mrs. Boone were still busy elsewhere. Theo checked his bike for further damage, and finding none, took off with Judge in hot pursuit.

Ike's office was on the second floor of an old building owned by a Greek couple. The first floor was their small deli, and the office above it was always engulfed in the smell of lamb roasting in onions. To a visitor, it was a heavy shot to the nose, though not altogether unpleasant, but Ike, after many years there, seemed not to notice the aroma.

Ike was at his long, cluttered desk, sipping a bottle of beer, listening to a barely audible Bob Dylan on the stereo, when Theo walked in without knocking and fell into a dusty old chair. "How's my favorite nephew," Ike asked, the same opening question each week. Theo was Ike's only nephew. Ha-ha.

"Great," Theo replied. "Kinda bummed out about the trial."

"Strange, indeed. I've been listening all day and have heard nothing."

Since his dramatic fall from a prominent and well-respected lawyer to a disbarred and eccentric old hippie, Ike had lived on the fringes of the underworld in Strattenburg, and down there he heard plenty. In one poker club, he played cards with retired cops and lawyers. In another, he rubbed elbows with several ex-criminals like himself. Regardless of the raging story, Ike could usually track down a rumor and examine it closely before it made its wider rounds.

"So what's your theory?" Ike asked.

Theo shrugged as if he knew precisely what happened. "It's simple, Ike. Pete Duffy hopped on a bike sometime after midnight, rode it a couple miles down a gravel road, hooked up with his accomplice, tossed his bike in the trunk of a car or the back of a pickup, and away they went." Theo delivered this quick narrative casually, as if he knew exactly how things had happened, and when he finished he offered a silent word of thanks to Mr. Mount.

Ike's eyes narrowed as he absorbed this. His jaw dropped slightly as he thought about it. His forehead wrinkled as he analyzed it. "Where did you hear that?" he asked.

"Hear it? Nowhere. I think it's obvious what happened. How else can you explain it?"

Ike scratched his beard and stared across the table. He was often impressed by the maturity and street savvy of his nephew, but this easy explanation of the Duffy mystery seemed a bit rehearsed. Theo decided to continue: "And I'll bet they don't find him. I'll bet Pete Duffy planned this perfectly and is now somewhere far away, probably with plenty of cash and a new set of ID papers."

"Oh really."

"Sure, Ike. He had an eight-hour head start, and the police have no idea what kind of vehicle he's in. So, what are they looking for? They don't know."

"You want something to drink?" Ike asked as he turned in his swivel chair. There was a small refrigerator under the credenza behind his desk and it was usually well stocked.

"No thanks," Theo said.

Ike pulled out another bottle of beer, popped the top, and took a sip. Theo knew that he drank too much, which he had learned by listening carefully around the offices at Boone & Boone, and around the courthouse as well. Two or three times he had picked up on comments that suggested Ike Boone struggled with the bottle, and Theo assumed this was true. However, he had never witnessed it. Ike was divorced and far removed from his children and grandchildren. He lived alone, and was, in Theo's opinion, a sad old man.

"Do you still have a B in Chemistry?" Ike asked.

"Come on, Ike. Do we have to discuss my grades all the time? They get enough attention from my parents. And it's an A minus, not a B."

"How are your parents?"

"They're doing fine. I have a note from my mother reminding me to ask you to join us for dinner tonight at Robilio's."

"How nice of her." Ike waved his hand over the files stacked haphazardly on his desk, then delivered the same, tired old line Theo heard almost daily from his own parents: "I have too much work."

What a surprise, thought Theo. For reasons he would never understand, the relationship between his parents and Ike was complicated, and there was nothing he could do to simplify things. "It doesn't take long to eat dinner," he said.

"Tell Marcella I said thanks."

"Will do."

Theo often confided in Ike, and told him things he would not tell his own parents. He considered mentioning how bizarre his day had become after leaving the courtroom that morning, but decided to let it pass. He could always tell Ike later, and seek his advice.

They talked baseball and football, and after half an hour Theo and Judge said good-bye. His bike was right where he had left it, with two tires full of air, and he dashed away with Judge following. He found both of his parents back at the office and went through the routine of briefly describing his day.

Marcella Boone did not enjoy cooking and was often too busy to even attempt it. Woods Boone was a lousy cook, but a fine eater, and since Theo was a toddler the family enjoyed sampling the wonderful ethnic foods of Strattenburg. On Monday, they ate Italian at Robilio's. Tuesday was soup and a sandwich in a homeless shelter, not exactly fine cuisine. They bounced back Wednesday with Chinese carryout from one of three restaurants they liked. On Thursday, Mr. Boone picked up the daily special at a Turkish deli. Friday dinner was always fish at Malouf's, a rowdy Lebanese bistro. On Saturday, they rotated selections, with each of the three picking their preference without input from the other two. Finally, on Sunday, Mrs. Boone would assume command of her kitchen and try a new recipe for a roasted chicken. The results were not always spectacular.

Precisely at 7:00 p.m., the Boone family entered Robilio's and were led to their favorite table.

Chapter 5

Tuesday morning. And not just any Tuesday, but the first Tuesday of the month, which meant Theo, and about fifty other Boy Scouts from Troop 1440, Old Bluff Council, wore their official scouting shirts and colorful neckerchiefs to school. The school board had decided that the wearing of a full uniform by a Boy Scout on school property would not be tolerated. There was a dress code that was vague, loosely enforced, and always causing trouble, and a full Scout uniform would not violate it. However, the school board was worried that if it allowed Boy Scout and Girl Scout uniforms on campus, even for just one specific day each month, then all types of uniforms might follow. Sports uniforms, karate uniforms, theatrical costumes, even religious garments like Buddhist robes and Muslim burkas. The entire issue had become complicated, and when a compromise was reached, Theo and the other Scouts felt lucky to get a partial uniform one day a month.

He showered quickly, brushed his teeth, which were covered in thick braces and virtually unseen, and put on his official khaki short-sleeved shirt adorned with the required council shoulder patch, blue-and-white troop numerals, patrol emblem, and Life Ranking Award. When the shirt was perfect and tucked into a pair of jeans, he carefully fitted the orange neckerchief around his neck and secured it with the official Scout slide. A full uniform would have allowed Theo to show off his merit badge sash, something he was proud of because he had just been awarded his twenty-second and twenty-third merit badges, for astronomy and golf. If all went according to plan, Theo would attain the rank of Eagle the summer before he entered the ninth grade. His goal, other than becoming an Eagle Scout, was to have at least thirty-five merit badges, all colorfully displayed and sewed on in perfect order by his mother.

Judge, who slept under Theo's bed, had been awake for thirty minutes and was tired of waiting. He was whimpering and wanted to go downstairs, then outside. Theo adjusted his neckerchief again, approved of what he saw in the mirror, grabbed his backpack, and bounced down the stairs.

For the moment, he had forgotten about the Pete Duffy disappearance.

His mother, who was not an early morning go-getter, was sipping coffee at the kitchen table and reading the newspaper. "Good morning, Theo. Aren't you cute?"

"Good morning," Theo said as he kissed his mother on the forehead. He hated the word "cute" when she used it to describe him. He opened the door and Judge disappeared outside. Before his chair was the usual—a box of cereal, a carton of milk, a bowl, a spoon, and a glass of orange juice.

"No sign of Pete Duffy," his mother said, her nose still stuck in the paper.

"They're not going to find him," Theo said, repeating what he had said numerous times over dinner.

"I'm not so sure about that. It's hard to run away from the FBI these days, with all the technology they have." Theo had heard this, too, over dinner. He fixed his bowl of cereal, then opened the door again so Judge could race in. Judge did not waste time in the mornings when breakfast was being served. Theo poured cereal and milk into the dog bowl, and Judge attacked it.

Without taking her eyes off the newspaper, Mrs. Boone said, "So you have scouting this afternoon, huh?"

No, Mom, it's Halloween.

No, Mom, all of my other shirts are dirty.

No, Mom, this is an attempt to confuse you so that you'll only think it's the first Tuesday of the month, then maybe you'll show up in the wrong courtroom.

Oh, all the things he wanted to say, but Theo, being a good Scout and respecting authority, and also being a good son and not wanting to anger his mother with a smart remark, said, "Sure."

"When is the next camping trip?" she asked, slowly turning a page.

"A week from Friday, at Lake Marlo." Troop 1440 spent at least one weekend per month in the woods, and the camping trips were Theo's favorite adventures.

There was at least one clock in every room of the Boone home, a clear sign of organized people. The one in the kitchen gave the time at 7:55, and Theo finished breakfast every day at 8:00 a.m. When Judge slurped his last bit of breakfast, Theo rinsed both bowls in the sink, returned the milk and orange juice to the refrigerator, then raced up the stairs where he stomped around his room a few times to make some noise. Without brushing his teeth for a second time, he sprinted back to the kitchen where he pecked his mother on the cheek and said, "I'm off to school."

"Lunch money?" she asked.

"Always."

"Is your homework done?"

"It's perfect, Mom. I'll see you after school."

"Be careful, Teddy, and remember to smile."

"I'm smiling, Mom."

"Love you, Teddy."

Over his shoulder he said, "Love you, Mom."

Outside, he rubbed Judge's head and said good-bye. Racing away, he repeated the word "Teddy," a bothersome little family nickname that he despised. "Cute little Teddy," he mumbled to himself. He waved at Mr. Nunnery, a neighbor who would spend his entire day sitting on his porch.

As Theo sped through Strattenburg, he remembered yesterday's incident in Buck Baloney's backyard, and decided to stay on the streets and obey the rules of the road. He also thought about the Duffy trial, and all the excitement he would miss because the defendant had chosen to become a fugitive. Theo thought about a lot of things as he dashed along the sleepy streets of Strattenburg. His locker—he was anxious to see if it had been violated. His slashed tire—could it possibly happen again? Omar Cheepe and Paco—might they still be watching him?

Homeroom was buzzing with the latest Duffy gossip.

All sixteen boys were brimming with opinions and scenarios they had picked up over the dinner table and heard their parents debating. One report had a possible sighting not far away by a rural mail carrier; another had Pete Duffy murdered by drug lords; yet another had him safe and untouchable in Argentina. Theo listened to the chatter but did not participate. He was just happy he had found his locker secure.

The bell rang and the boys filed out of the room and drifted to the hallway, another dreary day of classes underway.

Troop 1440 met in the basement of a building owned by the VFW (Veterans of Foreign Wars). Upstairs, the older soldiers gathered each afternoon for pinochle, cribbage, and beer, and on the first and third Tuesdays the Boy Scouts met below for their official meetings.

The scoutmaster was a former Marine who preferred to be called Major Ludwig, or simply Major for short. (And occasionally "Wiggie" behind his back, but only when it was absolutely certain that he was far away.) Major Ludwig was about sixty years old and ran Troop 1440 as if he were preparing a bunch of Marines for an invasion. He was a serious runner, claimed to do five hundred sit-ups and push-ups before breakfast, and was constantly pushing his boys to swim farther, row faster, hike longer, and, in general, do everything better. He monitored their report cards and expected every member of the troop to attain the rank of Eagle. He tolerated no bad habits and was quick to call parents if a Scout was falling behind. And, though he could bark like a drill sergeant, the Major knew precisely how to mix discipline and fun. He liked to yell, but he also liked to laugh. The boys adored him.

Occasionally, when he wasn't dreaming of becoming a great trial lawyer or a wise judge, Theo thought about becoming a full-time scoutmaster, just like the Major. Such a future posed problems, though, because scouting was volunteer work.

At precisely 4:00 p.m., the Major called for order and the large room fell silent. Troop 1440 was divided into five patrols—Panther, Rattlesnake, Ranger, Warthog, and Falcon. Each had a patrol leader, assistant leader, and seven or eight other members. Theo led the Falcon patrol. At rapt attention, and under the intense gaze of the Major, the troop pledged allegiance to the flag, then said the Scout pledge and motto. After the Scouts were seated, the Major led them through a well-organized agenda that included reports from each patrol, rankings and merit badge updates, fund-raising activities, and, most importantly, plans for the next weekend campout at Lake Marlo. There was a fifteen-minute video on first aid for puncture wounds, and that was followed by a work session with ropes and knots. The Major explained that he was less than impressed with the troop's overall level of hitching, lashing, and knotting, and he expected better work during the camping trip. Because he had been practicing for years, the Major was a whiz with the square knot and clove hitch, but what dazzled the boys was his mastery of the more complicated knots such as the timber hitch and overhand bend.

As always, the ninety-minute meeting flew by, and at precisely 5:30 it was adjourned. Most of the Scouts left on bikes, and as Theo shoved off with the gang, he realized there was a problem.

The rear tire was flat.

Gil's Wheels was closing as Theo approached, tired and sweating from the ordeal of pushing his bike at least ten blocks from the VFW. "Well, well," Gil said as he rubbed his hands on a shop rag he kept in a front pocket. "My favorite customer."

Theo felt like crying. Not only was he tired, but he was overwhelmed with the thought of buying another tire and, more importantly, frightened that someone was really after him. Gil spun the rear tire, stopped it, poked at the incision, and said, "Yep, probably the same knife that got the front tire yesterday. This happen at school?"

"No, at the VFW, while I was in a Scout meeting."

"So this person is following you around, huh?"

"I don't know, Gil. What should I do?"

"Have you told your parents?"

"No one knows but you."

Gil had a wrench and was slowly removing the rear tire from the bike's frame. "Me, I'd start with my parents, then I'd think about filing a report with the police. And someone at the school should know about it, too. I'll bet you're not the only kid who's getting his tires cut like this."

"Have you seen others in here?"

"Not in a couple of weeks, but this isn't the only bike shop in town. Of course, it's the best, if you want my unbiased opinion." Ha-ha. Gil laughed at his own humor, but Theo could not crack a smile.

"Eighteen dollars?" he asked.

"Same as yesterday," Gil replied.

"I guess I'd better talk to my dad."

"Good idea."

Woods Boone was in his office meeting with another lawyer. Marcella Boone was in her office with a divorce client. Elsa was on the phone when Theo arrived, and Dorothy and Vince were running errands. Only Judge was waiting for Theo, and the two made their way to his tiny office in the back of the building. Theo unloaded his backpack, and his desk—an old card table—was soon covered with books, notepads, and his laptop. He was daydreaming, though, and unable to concentrate on homework.

Why would anyone slash his tires and vandalize his locker? He had no known enemies, at that point in his life, unless he considered Omar Cheepe and Paco, and he was convinced they had more important things to worry about. They were career thugs, real pros, not exactly the types to do their dirty work around a middle school. How could they possibly sneak through the hallways of the school without being noticed? There was no way. And, why would they be interested in stealing a three-pack of inhalers and a Twins cap? He could not imagine them loitering around the bike racks by the front flagpole, watching for the right moment to cut his tire, or following him to the VFW for a Boy Scout meeting.

Theo suspected the vandal was another student. But who, and why? Theo was lost in these thoughts when, literally, his world was shattered.

There was a door that led from his office to the rear

parking lot of Boone & Boone, and the top half of the door was comprised of four panes of glass. A large rock suddenly burst through the glass, crashing loudly and sending shards of broken glass everywhere—onto the bookshelves, over his desk, across the floor. Judge jumped and barked loudly. Theo instinctively threw both arms over his head in case there was another rock on the way. He waited for a few seconds, trying to catch his breath, then bolted to his feet. He yanked open the door but saw no one outside. Judge, growling and barking, jumped down the steps and raced around the small parking lot, but found nothing.

The rock was the size of a softball and came to rest next to Judge's bed. Elsa rushed in and exclaimed, "Theo, what in the world!" Then she saw the shattered windowpanes and broken glass. "Are you okay!?"

"I think so," Theo said, still in shock.

"What happened?"

"Someone threw a rock," Theo said as he picked it up. They examined it. Mrs. Boone appeared and asked, "What's going on back here?" Then Mr. Boone walked in behind her and asked the same thing. For a few minutes they inspected the damage and scratched their heads. Elsa found a piece of glass in Theo's hair, but there were no wounds.

"I'll call the police," Mr. Boone said.

"Good idea," said Mrs. Boone.

"Any idea who did this?" Elsa asked.

"No," Theo replied.

Chapter 6

t was proving to be an eventful afternoon. Because Mrs. Boone handled a lot of divorces, and always on the side of the wife, the office was occasionally the scene of some bad family drama. Just as the dust had settled in Theo's office, and as Mr. Boone was heading toward the conference room to call the police, there were loud voices near the front door. An angry man and a shrieking woman were having a spat, and it quickly led to a confrontation. The woman was Mrs. Treen, a new Boone & Boone divorce client, and the man was her husband, Mr. Treen. They had a house full of kids and a world of problems, and Mrs. Boone had been trying to convince them to undergo marriage counseling instead of going the divorce route. According to Mrs. Treen, her husband had become violent and abusive and impossible to be around.

He certainly appeared to be violent as he stood by Elsa's desk and growled at his wife. "You are not filing for divorce! Over my dead body." He was a thick, stout man with a beard and eyes that flashed when he spoke. Mrs. Boone, Elsa, and Theo entered the reception area and stopped to watch.

Mr. Boone took a step forward and said, "Let's take a deep breath here and try to be civilized." Mrs. Treen eased away and stood close to Mrs. Boone. Elsa and Theo stayed in the background, all eyes and ears.

"I can't live with you," Mrs. Treen said. "I'm tired of getting punched and slapped around. I'm taking the kids and leaving, Roger, and there's nothing you can do about it."

"I've never hit you," he replied, though no one believed this. Mr. Treen had the look of a brawler who might slap just about anyone.

"Stop the lying, Roger," she said.

"Perhaps we should step into my office," Mrs. Boone said calmly.

"He's got a gun," Mrs. Treen said, and all spines stiffened. "It's in his pocket." All eyes went straight to the pockets of Mr. Treen's pants, and, sure enough, there appeared to be something dangerous there.

"Get in the car, Karen," Mr. Treen said with eyes glowing and jaw muscles clenching. No one with any sense would get in the car with this guy.

"No," she replied. "I'm not taking orders from you anymore."

"I'll ask you to leave," Mr. Boone said firmly.

Mr. Treen smiled, touched his right pocket, and said, "Maybe I don't want to leave."

"Then I'll call the police," Mr. Boone said.

There was a long pause. No one moved. Finally, Mrs. Boone said, "I have an idea. Let's step into the conference room, just the four of us, get some coffee, and have a conversation." Because she negotiated divorce settlements and spent a lot of time in the courtroom, Mrs. Boone understood the need for compromise. Her soft voice and even temper drained some of the tension.

It was a standoff. Mr. Treen was not leaving. Mrs. Treen was not leaving with him. And no one wanted to provoke the guy with the gun. Mr. Treen blinked first, and in doing so kept the situation from getting worse. He said, "Okay, let's talk."

Elsa quickly added, "I'll get the coffee."

The Treens and the Boones stepped into the conference room and closed the doors. At first Theo and Elsa were not sure if they should call the police or wait on Mr. Boone. Theo was worried about his parents being in there with a somewhat agitated and emotional man who was unstable enough to carry a pistol in his pocket. What if things took a turn for the worse? What if they suddenly heard gunfire popping in the conference room? Theo wanted to call the police immediately.

Elsa, though, had a different approach. Mr. Treen had agreed to talk peacefully about their problems. If the police showed up and arrested him on some weapons charge, then he might crack, go off the deep end, and do something crazier the next time. Elsa was confident her bosses could defuse the situation and perhaps make progress in settling some of the Treens' issues.

Elsa called a glass repairman who advertised 24-hour service.

Minutes passed with no gunfire from the conference room. Nor were there loud, angry voices. Theo settled down somewhat, though given the events of the day, he was still unnerved. He and Elsa decided to take photos of the office and show the police later. They swept up the glass and saved the rock for evidence. The repairman arrived after dark and began replacing the broken panes.

———————

Usually, on Tuesday nights, the Boones left their offices and walked a few blocks to the Highland Street Shelter where they served food to the homeless and helped in other ways. Mrs. Boone, along with three other female attorneys in Strattenburg, had started a small, free legal clinic for abused women, several of whom were homeless and stayed at the shelter. Mr. Boone saw clients there, too, typically folks who had been wrongfully evicted from their homes and apartments, and people who had been denied benefits. Theo's job was to help the homeless children with their studies.

The meeting with the Treens gave every indication of lasting forever, so Theo decided to go to the shelter alone. His parents would catch up later, if for no other reason than to have dinner. After they served the homeless, they always had a quick bowl of soup or a sandwich before dispensing legal advice. Theo was starving and tired of the office. He said good-bye to Elsa and rode his bike to the shelter. He was too late for dinner but found leftovers in the kitchen.

His current project was teaching Math to the Koback boys. Russ was eight and Ben was seven, and they had been living in the shelter with their mother for the past two months. Mrs. Boone was handling the legal matters for Mrs. Koback, and, though Theo did not know the details, he did know the little family was reeling from some type of tragedy. Mr. Koback had been killed in a faraway place, and in a manner that was not being discussed. After he died, the family lost everything and had lived in an old truck for several weeks before finding beds in the shelter.

For Theo's Eagle Scout project, he was planning to organize a program in which teenage volunteers who were old enough to drive would adopt a homeless kid, sort of like Big Brothers–Big Sisters. He was also thinking about building another shelter, one that would house homeless people who were still living in tents and under bridges. However, his father had warned him that such a project would cost millions.

As usual, the Koback boys were subdued, even shy. Their young lives had been filled with turmoil and misery. Mrs. Boone said they were damaged and needed counseling. Theo managed to coax a few smiles as they plowed through the Math workbooks. Their mother sat nearby, watching, and, as Theo suspected, trying to learn the Math, too. Theo knew she could not read well.

Each visit to the shelter reminded Theo how fortunate he was. Only half a mile from his warm, secure environment, there were people like the Kobacks, sleeping on cots in a shelter and eating food donated by churches and charities. Theo's future was fairly predictable. If all went according to plan, he would finish high school, go to college (he had not yet decided where), then on to law school to become a lawyer. The Koback boys, on the other hand, had no idea where they would be living in a year. Highland Street allowed its "friends" to stay for twelve months only, during which time they were expected to find a job and a more permanent place to live. So, like everyone else, the Kobacks were just passing through.

At 9:00 p.m., all volunteers checked out of the shelter. Theo said good-bye to Ben, Russ, and their mother, and left the basement. There was no sign of his parents, so he decided to bike back to the office to get his backpack and his dog, and hopefully find everyone still alive. There was almost no traffic at that hour, and Theo darted through the streets with little regard for the rules of the road. He jumped curbs, dashed along sidewalks, ran STOP signs, and along the way reminded himself of how nice it was to have two fully inflated tires.

At the corner of Main and Farley, a red light had two cars waiting in front of Theo, so he swerved onto the sidewalk. As he was executing a rather risky sliding turn onto Main, he slid into another bike, one being ridden by a uniformed policeman—Officer Stu Peckinpaw, a lean, gray-haired veteran who'd been patrolling downtown Strattenburg for decades. Every kid in town knew him, and tried to avoid him.

Theo bounced up, unhurt, and brushed the dirt off his legs. "Sorry about that," he said, half expecting to be arrested and hauled away to the police station.

Officer Peckinpaw leaned his bike against a signpost and removed his helmet. "What's your name, kid?" he demanded, as if Theo might be a serial killer.

"Theo Boone." The two had met several times over the years, at least in passing. This, though, was Theo's first real run-in with Officer Stu.

"That name's familiar," he said, and gave Theo the opening he always wanted.

"Yes, sir. My dad is Woods Boone and my mother is Marcella Boone. The law firm of Boone & Boone."

"Rings a bell. So, if both parents are lawyers, then you should know the law, right?"

"I guess."

"City code prohibits bikes on sidewalks at all hours of the day and night, no exceptions. Don't you know this?"

"Yes, sir, I do."

Peckinpaw glared at Theo as if he might whip out the old handcuffs and slap both wrists together. "Are you okay?"

"Yes, sir."

"Then get home and stay off the sidewalks."

"Yes, sir. Thanks."

Officer Stu had the reputation of having a loud bark but no bite, and he rarely wrote tickets to kids on bikes. He liked to yell and threaten, but preferred to avoid the paperwork. Theo sped away, greatly relieved to be out of trouble, but also curious about what else might happen on this eventful day. His cell phone beeped and he stopped to answer it. It was his mother, telling him to head home. The meeting with the Treens was finally over, and it had been a success.

His parents were eating a frozen pizza when he walked into the kitchen. They were exhausted. They asked about the shelter, but were almost too tired to talk. Theo was curious about the Treens and what happened after he left, but the old attorney-client shield was quickly thrown up and the conversation was cut off. His parents never talked about their clients. Never. A client's business and the conversation between lawyers and their clients were strictly off-limits. Mrs. Boone did say an agreement had been reached, and the Treens would seek counseling.

Theo had a lot of things to discuss. Two punctured tires, a vandalized school locker, now a rock through his office window. Someone was tormenting him and he needed to talk. But it would be a long conversation, and all the Boones, including Judge, were ready for bed. His father, a lawyer who usually avoided conflict, seemed especially fatigued by the three-hour ordeal with the Treens. Mrs. Boone was complaining of a headache. Theo was about to press on anyway because he needed help and advice, but just as he was about to say something, the phone rang. It was Mrs. Treen, upset again.

Theo and Judge went upstairs to bed.

Chapter 7

The following day, Wednesday, Theo raced to school as always, though he did avoid downtown, and he did stay off the sidewalks. He did not have the chance to chat with his parents over breakfast because his father, as always, left for early gossip with his coffee group and his mother was walking out the door, late for a meeting. Theo and Judge ate alone and in silence.

According to the headlines, there was no sign of Pete Duffy. Thieves had broken into a computer store on Main Street. Two students at Stratten College had been arrested for cyber stalking. Not a single word about some unknown thug vandalizing the law office of Theo Boone, since the police had yet to be notified.

Theo was thankful for Wednesday; it would certainly be better than Tuesday.

During second period Geometry, Theo's Wednesday suddenly became much worse than his Tuesday. Over the loudspeaker, the shrieking voice of the school secretary, Miss Gloria, demanded, "Miss Garman, is Theo Boone present?"

At that moment, Theo was drifting away and daydreaming about the upcoming camping trip to Lake Marlo. At the sound of his name, he bolted upright and felt as though he'd been slapped.

"He is," Miss Garman replied.

"Send him to the office, please."

Theo jumped to his feet and left the room.

There were two detectives in dark suits sitting in the office of the principal, Mrs. Gladwell, who looked like she had seen a ghost when Theo walked in. She gushed, "Theo, these two gentlemen are with the police department and they would like to talk to you." Neither detective stood, neither smiled. The short one was an older man, a Detective Vorman, and Theo had seen him around the courthouse. In fact, Theo had watched him testify in a trial a couple of months earlier. The other, Detective Hamilton, Theo had never seen before. He said, "Theo, we'd like to ask you a few questions."

Since there were no empty chairs, Theo leaned with his back against the wall and wondered why they were there. His first thought was the broken window, but he quickly dismissed it. Such a minor act of vandalism would not require the involvement of two detectives. Theo managed to say, "Okay."

Hamilton went on, "Did you happen to be downtown last night?"

Theo did not like his tone, nor his frown. Combined, they gave the strong impression that they suspected him of doing something wrong. Theo looked at Mrs. Gladwell, who was nervously tapping her fingers on her desk. He looked at Detective Vorman who was writing something on his pocket notepad.

Theo said, "I was at the Highland Street Shelter last night."

"Were you on Main Street for any reason last night?" Hamilton asked.

"Why are you asking me these questions?" Theo asked, and this really irritated both detectives.

"I'll handle the questions, Theo. You do the answers," Hamilton sneered like a bad TV actor.

"Just answer the questions," Vorman chimed in, a real bully.

"No, I was not downtown," Theo said slowly. "I went to the shelter, then I rode my bike home."

"Did you bump into Officer Stu Peckinpaw?" Hamilton asked.

"Yes. I accidentally ran into him, but everything was okay."

"And where did this take place?"

"On Main Street, Main and Farley."

"So you were downtown last night, weren't you, Theo?"

"I was on my bike."

The detectives gave each other a smug look. Mrs. Gladwell tapped her fingers even faster. Hamilton said, "There's a computer store on Main Street, two blocks down from Farley. It's called Big Mac's Systems. You know the place?"

Theo shook his head. No. However, he remembered the name from his quick review of the morning's local headlines. The store had been broken into the night before.

Vorman helped out. "They sell PCs, laptops, printers, software, the usual, but also the latest tablets, SmartPads, e-book readers, even cell phones. You've never been to the store, Theo?"

"No, sir."

"Do you have a laptop?"

"Yes, sir. Jupiter Air, thirteen inch. Got it for Christmas."

"Where is it now?"

"In my backpack, back in the classroom."

"Do you ever keep it in your locker?" Hamilton asked.

"Occasionally. Why?"

"Again, Theo, we'll handle the questions."

"Okay, but I get the feeling you think I've done something wrong. And, if that's the case, then I want to call a lawyer."

Both detectives found this amusing. A thirteen-year-old kid asking for a lawyer. They dealt with thugs and criminals all day long, and every one of them demanded a lawyer. This kid must watch too much television.

"We'd like to see your locker," Hamilton said.

Theo knew it was unwise to agree to any type of search. Car, home, pockets, office, even locker—never agree to a search. If the police believed there was evidence of a crime, then they could go to a judge and get a warrant, or written permission, and conduct a search. However, Theo knew he had done nothing wrong and, like all innocent people, wanted to prove this to the police. He also knew the school could open his locker without his approval.

"Sure," he said, somewhat reluctantly, and both detectives, as well as Mrs. Gladwell, could not help but notice that Theo hesitated before agreeing to a search. The four left the office and headed down the empty hallway. The bell would ring in less than fifteen minutes, and there would be plenty of students to witness Theo in the presence of two dark-suited strangers. Within seconds the entire school would know that he was being investigated for something. When they stopped in front of his locker, Theo glanced around. The hall was empty.

"When did you last open your locker?" Hamilton asked.

"When I got to school this morning. Around eight thirty."

"So, about two hours ago."

"Yes, sir."

"And did you notice anything unusual at that time?"

"No, sir." Theo wanted to mention the fact that a stranger had been in his locker on Monday, but he was suddenly in a hurry. He was terrified that someone might see him with two cops and the principal.

"You can open it now," Hamilton said.

Theo punched in the code—58343 (Judge)—and pulled open the door. Nothing appeared to be missing, but something had certainly been added. On the left side, leaning against some textbooks, were three slender objects Theo had never seen before.

"Don't touch anything," Hamilton said as he leaned down and in and breathed on Theo's neck. Vorman and Mrs. Gladwell huddled close, and for a few seconds no one moved or said a word. Finally, Hamilton asked, "See anything unusual, Theo?"

With a dry mouth, Theo managed to say, "Yes, sir. Those are not mine."

The slender objects were Linx 0-4 Tablets, the hottest and lightest personal computers dominating the marketplace. With stunning graphics, unlimited memory, a million applications, and a price tag of $399, the 0-4 was cheaper, yet far more sophisticated than its current competition. Detective Vorman, wearing surgical gloves and treating the 0-4s like rare diamonds, placed them side by side on Mrs. Gladwell's desk. Big Mac had been called and was on his way to identify his stolen property.

"Please call my mother," Theo said to Mrs. Gladwell. "Or my father. It doesn't matter."

"Not so fast," Hamilton said. "We have some more questions."

"I'm not answering any more questions," Theo said. "I want my parents here."

"If Theo says he didn't steal these tablets, then I believe him," Mrs. Gladwell said.

"Thank you so much," Hamilton said.

"How did you know they were there?" Theo asked.

"And once again, young Theo, please, we'll handle the questions," Hamilton said. His tone and attitude had been lousy to start with; now, with the evidence in hand and the crime apparently solved, he was becoming unbearable.

"Can I call his parents?" Mrs. Gladwell asked.

"Sure you can," Theo said. "They don't run this school. They can't tell you what to do."

"Knock it off, kid," Vorman said.

"I beg your pardon!" Mrs. Gladwell said. "Don't talk to my student in such a manner. Theo is no criminal. I believe whatever he says."

Theo walked to a spot beside Mrs. Gladwell, who was seated at her desk, and removed his cell phone. Using speed dial, he called the offices of Boone & Boone. Elsa answered, and Theo, staring straight into the angry eyes of Detective Hamilton said, "Hey, Elsa, it's me, Theo. I need to talk to Mom."

"Something wrong, Theo?"

"No. Just let me talk to Mom."

"She's in court, Theo. She'll be tied up all morning."

"Okay, then let me talk to Dad."

"He's not here. He's in Wilkesburg closing a land deal. What's going on, Theo?"

Theo did not have the time to chat with Elsa, and she could not help him anyway. The detectives were fuming and Theo figured he was almost out of time. He canceled the call to Elsa, punched another number for speed dial, and said, "Ike, it's me, Theo."

Ike replied, "Good morning, Theo. Why are you calling me at ten thirty?"

Theo said, "Ike, I'm at school and there are two detectives here accusing me of stealing computers that someone put in my locker. Can you get down here?"

"That's enough, kid," Hamilton growled. Ike did not respond but his office line went dead.

Theo slapped his phone shut and returned it to his pocket. Technically, this was a violation of school rules. Only eighth graders were allowed to have phones on campus, and a few of them did. Their use was strictly controlled. All cell phones had to be turned off during classes and could be used only during recess and lunch. Under the circumstances, though, Theo doubted if Mrs. Gladwell would be upset with him. She was not.

"We haven't accused you of anything," Hamilton said. "We're just doing our investigation, and when we find stolen goods in someone's possession, then we have to ask questions. Doesn't that make sense?"

"Theo didn't steal the computers, okay?" Mrs. Gladwell said firmly.

Vorman decided to play the nice cop and offered a sappy smile. "So, Theo, if you didn't place these computers in your locker, then someone else obviously did. Who else has the entry code to your locker?"

Safe question. Theo replied, "No one that I know of, but someone was in my locker Monday. They stole a Twins baseball cap and some other items. I didn't report it at that time, but I was planning to."

Mrs. Gladwell turned and looked at Theo. "You should have told us, Theo."

"I know, I know. I'm sorry. I was going to discuss it with my parents first, then report it to you, but I never got the time."

"And the school has a list of all entry codes?" Vorman asked.

"Yes, but it's protected in a secure file in our main computer," Mrs. Gladwell said.

"Has anyone ever hacked into it?"

"Not to my knowledge."

"Has the school had a problem with people breaking into lockers?"

"No," she replied. "Occasionally a student will fail to

properly close a locker, and the door will be left slightly open. This might lead to a missing item or two, but I cannot recall a situation where a student obtained an entry code and went into another student's locker."

"How about you, Theo?" Vorman asked. "Do you know of anyone who got somebody else's code and broke into their locker?"

"No, sir."

Hamilton glanced at his notes, then looked at Theo and said, "During the break-in last night at Big Mac's Systems, the thief or thieves took ten of these tablets, six fifteen-inch laptops, and about a dozen cell phones. You have any idea where this stuff is now?"

Theo gritted his teeth and said, "I don't know anything about the break-in last night because I wasn't there, and I don't know how these tablets got into my locker. I said I wanted to talk to a lawyer, and I'm not answering any more questions until my lawyer is present."

"Things will go smoother if you cooperate with us, Theo," Hamilton said.

"I am cooperating. I allowed you to search my locker, and I'm telling the truth."

Chapter 8

Big Mac was a small man, only slightly taller than Theo, and when he entered Mrs. Gladwell's office he glared at the suspect as if he wanted to shoot him. Theo stood his ground behind the principal's chair and watched as the detectives offered Big Mac a pair of surgical gloves.

"Why don't you two wait outside?" Hamilton said, and Theo and Mrs. Gladwell stepped outside into the reception area. When the door was shut, she said, quietly, "I don't know why they have to be so rude."

"They're just doing their job," Theo said.

"Do you want to call your parents again?"

"Maybe later. They're not in the office and they're busy."

The bell rang loudly, and Theo looked for a place to hide. Students would be changing classes, and it was not unusual for several of them to rush into the front office for urgent business. Someone might see him sitting there, looking guilty, detained for some reason. He found a magazine, hid his face behind it, and cowered near the watercooler as the noise from the halls rose through the school.

Inside Mrs. Gladwell's office, Big Mac removed a small plate on the back of each tablet and checked the registration numbers. Using gloves to avoid smudging any possible fingerprints, he compared the number to his inventory list. "Yep, these came from my store," he said. "Looks like you got your man."

"We'll see," Hamilton said.

"What do you mean by that? You found these in that kid's locker, right? Looks to me like you got him nailed, caught red-handed. I want to press charges right now. Let's put the squeeze on him so we can find all the other stuff he stole."

"We'll handle the investigation, Mac."

"I think I saw that kid in my store last week."

Vorman looked at Hamilton. "Are you sure about this, Mac?"

"I can't prove it, you know? A lot of kids come and go, but that one looks familiar."

"He told us he's never been in your store."

"What do you expect him to say? We know he's a thief,

don't we? If he'll break in and steal, then I'm sure he'll lie, too. I want that kid busted, okay? I lose a ton of money every year to shoplifters and thieves, and I prosecute everyone I catch."

"Got it, Mac. We'll wrap up the investigation and stop by the store when we're finished. Thanks for your cooperation."

"No problem. Just find the rest of my stuff, okay?"

"We'll do that."

Big Mac slammed the door to Mrs. Gladwell's office, and as he stomped past Miss Gloria's desk, he saw Theo hiding near the watercooler. "Hey you, kid, where's the rest of the stuff you stole from my store?" he demanded. At that moment, there was a sixth-grade teacher chatting quietly with Mrs. Gladwell not far away, and there was a seventh-grade student with a fever lying on a small sofa. Everyone looked at Big Mac, then at Theo, who couldn't speak for a second or two.

"I want my stuff, okay?" Big Mac said, even louder, and took a step toward Theo.

"I don't have it," Theo managed to say.

"If you don't mind," Mrs. Gladwell said to Big Mac. The door opened and Detective Vorman stepped out. He pointed a finger at Big Mac and said, "That's enough. We'll handle things here. You can go now." Big Mac left without another word.

The bell was ringing to start third period. The sixth-grade teacher was staring at Theo as if he were a murderer. Mark Somebody, the student with the fever, was sitting up, staring at Theo. Miss Gloria's eyebrows were arched, and her forehead was creased with thick wrinkles, a very guilty look. Theo wanted to shout that he was not a thief, had not stolen anything belonging to Big Mac, in fact had never stolen anything in his life, but for a few long seconds he just stood there in disbelief.

He had never before been accused of a crime.

Detective Vorman said, "Could you please come in?" Theo followed Mrs. Gladwell back into her office, where she sat in her large swivel chair behind her desk. Theo stood beside her; the two of them versus the two detectives.

Vorman said, "These were identified by the owner. Registration numbers match up all nice and neat. Now that we have recovered some of the stolen property, we need to thoroughly examine Mr. Boone's locker. Check it carefully for fingerprints. Inventory its contents. That sort of thing."

Hamilton chimed in, "And we'll need to talk to the kids who have lockers near this one. Maybe they saw something or someone suspicious, you know, just routine stuff. The sooner we can do this the better. Kids have short memories, you know."

Mrs. Gladwell knew that thirteen-year-olds have far better memories than adults, but she would not argue. She said, "Okay, but I'm certain you can wait until after three thirty this afternoon when classes are over. Why disrupt school during the day?"

Theo was horrified at the idea of the two detectives lining up his friends for questioning. Word would soon spread that Theo was under suspicion, that the cops were hot on his trail. Theo needed help. Mrs. Gladwell was doing her best to protect him, but Theo needed more firepower.

The door burst open and Ike stormed in. "What's going on here!?" he demanded. "Theo, are you okay?"

"Not really," Theo said.

Vorman stood and said, "I'm Detective Vorman, Strattenburg P.D. and this is my partner, Detective Hamilton. Who, may I ask, are you?" The introductions were stiff; none of the three men made any effort to shake hands.

"Ike Boone, formerly of Boone & Boone, attorneys, and Theo is my nephew."

"And I'm Mrs. Gladwell, the principal. Welcome to my office."

Ike nodded slightly and said, "A pleasure. I think we've met before. Now what's going on?"

"Are you a lawyer?" Vorman asked.

Ike replied, "Former lawyer. Right now I'm Theo's uncle,

adviser, consultant, guardian, and anything else I need to be. If you want lawyers, just give me an hour or so and I'll have them lined up." Ike was wearing his usual attire: faded jeans, sandals with no socks, an ancient Red Stripe Beer T-shirt under a ragged brown-plaid sports coat, and his long, gray hair was pulled back into a tight ponytail. He was highly agitated and looking for a fight, and Theo realized at that moment that he could have no better protector.

Detective Hamilton read the situation perfectly and took over. In a calm voice he said, "Fine, Mr. Boone. A computer store on Main Street was broken into last night. This morning we received an anonymous tip that some of the loot could be found in the locker of one Theodore Boone, here at the school. Theo consented to a search of his locker, and we found these three Linx 0-4 Tablets, valued at about four hundred dollars each. The owner of the store has checked the serial numbers and identified his goods."

"Perfect!" Ike said loudly. "Then we know exactly who robbed the store. The punk who gave you the anonymous tip. Why aren't you chasing him down instead of harassing Theo?"

"No harassment, Mr. Boone," Hamilton said. "We are merely conducting an investigation, part of which is an effort to track down the anonymous caller. We're trying to cover everything right now, okay?"

Ike took a breath and looked at his nephew. "Are you okay, Theo?"

"I guess," he replied, but he was not. Two slashed bike tires, a rock through his window with broken glass all over him and his dog, the first invasion into his locker and the stolen cap, and now this. Someone was tormenting him, and doing a fine job of it.

Mrs. Gladwell said, "Well if you want my opinion, and we are in my office so I'll just go ahead and give it anyway, the police have every right to pursue an investigation, as long as it does not disrupt my school. It's also my opinion that Theodore Boone didn't steal anything."

The three men nodded. Theo agreed completely but didn't move a muscle.

"What's next?" Ike snarled at the detectives.

Detective Hamilton replied, "Well, we would like Theo to come down to the police station so we can take a formal statement from him. Just a routine matter. Then we'd like to talk to some of the other students."

Theo had watched enough television to know that a trip downtown usually meant handcuffs and a ride in the back of the patrol car, and for a split second he was amused by the idea. He had never been handcuffed before, nor had he seen the backseat of a police car, and the entire adventure would be fun to talk about later, long after he was cleared.

But any amusement soon faded when he realized that the gossip would race through the school and the town and soon the whole world would know that Theo was the prime suspect.

"School's out at three thirty, right?" Ike asked Mrs. Gladwell.

"That's correct."

"Good. I'll have Theo at the police station at four o'clock this afternoon, if that suits you. I'm sure his parents will be with him."

The detectives exchanged glances, and it was obvious neither wanted to argue with Ike about this. "When can we have a chat with the other students?" Vorman asked.

"Well, I suppose at three thirty," Mrs. Gladwell said.

"Whose lockers are next to yours, Theo?" Hamilton asked.

"Woody, Chase, Joey, Ricardo, most of the guys in my homeroom," Theo replied. "Darren is directly below me."

Vorman looked at Hamilton and said, "We'll need to check with the lab and see if they can dust the area for fingerprints."

"Right," Hamilton replied. "And we'll need to print you, too, Theo. We can do it this afternoon when you come in."

"You want my fingerprints?" Theo asked.

"Of course."

"I'm not sure about that," Ike said. "I'll discuss it with his parents."

"I don't care," Theo said. "Take them. You won't find any of my prints on those tablets because I've never touched them. And if you want to you can give me a lie detector test, fine. I have nothing to hide."

"We'll see," Vorman said. The detectives were suddenly in a hurry to leave. Hamilton flipped his notepad shut and stuck it in a coat pocket. "Thank you for your time, Mrs. Gladwell," he said, standing. "And thanks, Theo, for your cooperation. Mr. Boone, it's been a real pleasure."

After they left, Theo sat down in the chair that Hamilton had used. "There's something else we need to talk about," he said, and Ike fell into the other chair. As Mrs. Gladwell listened intently, Theo described his two slashed tires, one of which happened on school property. When Theo recounted the story of the rock crashing into his office the day before, Ike said, "Someone's after you."

"No kidding," Theo said.

Chapter 9

Not surprisingly, the situation changed dramatically when Theo's mother got involved.

Theo called her during lunch, and fifteen minutes later she was at the school, in Mrs. Gladwell's office, demanding answers. She was furious that Theo had been interrogated by the police without his parents being present, but Mrs. Gladwell assured her that Theo handled himself well. He was cautious with his answers and gave the officers as little information as possible. The search of his locker was unavoidable because the school had the right to open it for any good reason. School policy required Mrs. Gladwell and all other administrators to fully cooperate with law enforcement officials in all situations.

Mrs. Boone initially wanted to take Theo from school,

to her office, and then to the police station. Mrs. Gladwell, though, thought it wiser to wait until classes were over. Theo had already been yanked out of class once that Wednesday, and to do so again would only create even more suspicion. Just keep things as normal as possible, she advised. Then she went on to discuss the rest of Theo's rather exciting week. Theo had not yet told his parents about his slashed tires and the first locker break-in, and his mother was shocked to learn of these episodes. She was more than a bit irritated that Theo had kept it all quiet.

As she was leaving, she asked Mrs. Gladwell to give Theo strict instructions to go straight to the office after school.

At 3:30, Detective Hamilton was waiting in Mr. Mount's classroom. He had called Mr. Mount and asked him to "invite" Darren, Woody, Chase, Joey, and Ricardo to hang around after school for a brief meeting. With Mr. Mount present, the detective spoke with each boy separately, and briefly. Darren was first, and after establishing the exact location of his locker in an enlarged photo, the detective asked, "What time did you first go to your locker this morning?"

Darren shrugged and said, "When I got to school, just before homeroom."

"And homeroom begins when?"

"Eight forty."

"Why did you go to your locker?"

"To get some books and drop off some books, same as always."

"Did you see Theo Boone at the locker this morning?"

Darren thought for a second, shrugged again, and said, "I don't think so. I think Theo was already in homeroom."

"Who do you remember seeing at your locker this morning?"

Another pause as he pondered the question. "Ricardo, maybe Woody. Just some of the guys. I really didn't stop and think about who I was seeing at the time. We're usually in a hurry to get to homeroom."

"Did you see anyone near the lockers who didn't belong there?" Hamilton asked slowly.

"Like who?"

"Like anybody who shouldn't have been hanging around your lockers?"

"Did somebody do something wrong?"

"That's what we're trying to find out, Darren. Did you see a stranger around the lockers at any time before ten o'clock this morning?"

"A stranger? Like an adult?"

"An adult, another student, anyone who would not normally be hanging around the locker area on this end of the hallway?"

Another, longer pause, then he slowly shook his head. "No, sir, I didn't see anyone like that."

"Nothing out of the ordinary?"

"No, sir."

Similar conversations were had with the other boys. Only Chase remembered bumping into Theo that morning at the lockers, and, no, Chase did not see Theo remove books or other items from his backpack. Detective Hamilton was careful not to reveal what had been found in Theo's locker, and he was careful not to give the impression that their friend was in hot water.

At 4:00 p.m. Wednesday afternoon, Theo and his parents, and Ike, too, walked into the police station on Main Street, two blocks east of the courthouse. They were met by Detective Vorman, who led them down a flight of stairs to a small room in the cramped basement. After offering them something to drink—all declined—Vorman got down to business. He and Mrs. Boone had already spoken twice by phone that afternoon, so there would be no surprises.

Theo would voluntarily give a statement, with plenty

of legal advice nearby, and Vorman would record it by video camera and audiotape. Theo had assured his parents that he had nothing to hide and knew nothing about the break-in or the stolen goods.

He began with Monday and the first episode with his locker. He covered the two slashed tires and said that Gil at Gil's Wheels could confirm those details. He explained, again, that he had not told his parents because he simply had not had the time or opportunity. He described the large rock crashing into his office the day before. With Vorman serving up easy questions, Theo finally got around to the stolen tablets in his locker. He had gone to his locker just a few minutes before homeroom, same as always. The hall was crowded, noisy, just like the day before and the day before that. He opened the locker with his code and saw nothing out of the ordinary. He was paying close attention to the contents of his locker because of what happened on Monday. He was certain the Linx Tablets were not in his locker at that time. He did not see anyone unusual hanging around—no strange adults, no students from other classes, grades, or classrooms. He was not aware of any other person with knowledge of his code. He did not know of similar incidents involving unauthorized entry into a locker at the school.

Theo spoke slowly and carefully, and repeated his

statements when asked to do so. To his left was his mother, to his right, his father. Ike was at the end of the table, still irritated that the police would dare suspect his nephew. Detective Hamilton sat directly across from Theo and patiently walked him through the process. A video camera on a tripod stood next to Hamilton and recorded it all.

Theo gave an accurate and detailed summary of his brief run-in with Officer Stu Peckinpaw Tuesday night, and explained the circumstances surrounding it. He was certain that he had never been inside Big Mac's Systems. He suggested they check the store's sales records to prove he had never bought anything there.

When he finished, the camera and recorder were turned off and everyone relaxed. Detective Hamilton explained that they would postpone the fingerprinting because there was not a single print taken from any of the three tablets. There was nothing to compare with Theo's prints. "Someone was very careful," Hamilton said, looking at Theo. "Wiped everything off, probably used gloves."

Theo was unable to tell if Hamilton still suspected him. Like all good detectives, he revealed little and acted as though anyone could be guilty.

"What about the anonymous caller," Ike asked. "Any luck tracing his call?"

"Sort of," Hamilton answered abruptly, and it was

obvious he did not want to be pressed by Ike. "It came from a pay phone near the hospital, so it will be difficult to determine who made the call."

"What time was it received?" asked Woods Boone.

"Nine twenty," Hamilton replied.

Mr. Boone continued: "So, if the tablets were not in Theo's locker at eight forty, when he stopped by, then the thief opened his locker at some point during the first period. After he dropped off the tablets, he either left the school and raced to a pay phone near the hospital and made the call, or he notified someone on the outside that the mission was accomplished and the police could then be notified. Probably the latter. So you have more than one member of some little gang at work here."

Detective Hamilton stared at Woods Boone, who stared right back. "Perhaps you should become a detective," Hamilton said.

"Perhaps you should see the obvious here. This was a plant. A setup. Don't know who or why, but it's pretty clear that Theo had nothing to do with it. Right now he's a victim, not a suspect."

"I haven't called him a suspect, Mr. Boone," Hamilton said coolly. "The crime is less than twenty-four hours old, give us a break here. We've just begun the investigation."

"What's next, as far as Theo is concerned?" asked Mrs. Boone.

"He's free to go. We're not going to arrest him in the middle of the night. If we need to have another chat, I'll give you a call." Hamilton was getting a bit testy, probably because he was getting grilled by a bunch of lawyers. "Our job is to track down all leads and try to determine who committed this crime. We don't know if Theo is telling the truth. He certainly sounds believable, but I'm a detective and I've talked to a lot of criminals who claimed to be innocent. Maybe he is, maybe he's not. You folks have no doubts, but that's not the way detectives go about their work. One day, soon we hope, we'll know a lot more, and then I'd like to be able to say, 'Theo, you're telling the truth.' Until that happens, though, I'm not believing anybody."

"You don't believe me?" Theo asked, wounded.

"Look, Theo, I don't know if you're lying, and I don't know if you're telling the truth. It's too early for me, as the detective handling the case, to make that decision. We don't have much evidence in this case, so far, but what we do have points to you. Do you understand this?"

Theo nodded slightly, but it was obvious he wasn't pleased with it.

Hamilton looked at his watch, closed a file, and said,

"Now, I thank you folks for stopping by, and, as I said, we'll be in touch."

The Boones walked out of the police building in a small group. No one was smiling.

Theo tried to study in his office at Boone & Boone, but he was too distracted. A new window had been installed, and the shattered glass had been removed. There was no sign of the damage from yesterday afternoon, but Theo could still hear the crash of the breaking glass, the sharp thud of the rock hitting the bookshelf, the splattering of debris, the shriek of panic from Judge, followed quickly by a furious round of barking in the frantic seconds afterward. Theo could almost hear something else. He thought he had heard it in a dream. He thought he had heard it once that morning at school during first period, before the police showed up and ruined his day. He could almost close his eyes, place himself at his desk when the rock came crashing through, and then, in the seconds that followed, he could almost hear footsteps. Someone was running away. The person who threw the rock was making his escape from close by. Theo wished a dozen times he had been able to catch a glimpse of the person running away.

Who was this mysterious person? Was it an adult?

Another student? Male or female? A lone gunman or a member of a gang?

Even Judge seemed a bit jumpy. The first return visit to the scene of the crime brings back bad memories, and Theo found it impossible to do his homework. He finally locked the door, took a peek through the new window, saw no one, and left the building on his bike, with Judge in hot pursuit.

Chapter 10

The photo was sent from an anonymous GashMail account, and initially sent to the in-boxes of a dozen or so students at Strattenburg Middle School. From there it rapidly picked up steam, and by 7:30 Wednesday evening hundreds, if not thousands, of people in town had seen it and knew what it was all about.

It was taken by a person who was determined to remain nameless and faceless, and, evidently, he or she was hiding somewhere across the street when Theo, his parents, and Ike left the police station. The photo clearly showed all four, frowning and worried, and just behind and above them, on the front of the building, in bold letters were the words: STRATTENBURG POLICE STATION.

With the photo was a description: "Theo Boone, age

thirteen, of 886 Mallard Lane, leaves the Strattenburg Police Station with his parents after being arrested for the Tuesday night break-in and burglary of the well-known downtown computer store, Big Mac's Systems. Sources say the police found stolen merchandise Wednesday morning in Boone's locker at the middle school. He is expected to appear in Juvenile Court next week."

As always on Wednesday evenings, the Boones were having Chinese takeout. They were in the den, dining on folding TV trays while watching television. Judge, who considered himself at least half human, was sitting next to Theo, getting an occasional bite of sweet-and-sour shrimp, his favorite. There was almost no conversation over dinner. Theo was burdened by recent events, which seemed to be snowballing. His parents were preoccupied with thoughts of protecting their son. Mrs. Boone hardly nibbled at her chicken chow mein. Mr. Boone chewed with a vengeance, as if he were off in court somewhere slugging it out with the bad guys and proving that Theo had done nothing wrong.

Theo's cell phone vibrated—a text message was arriving. He glanced at it. April Finnemore, his close friend, said: *TB, check email now. Urgent.*

Interrupting dinner was frowned on by his parents, so Theo, between bites, texted back: *What is it?*

April replied: *Terrible. Urgent! Go now.*

Theo replied: *OK.*

He took a few more bites, chewed, and swallowed quickly, then announced, "I'm stuffed." He stood with his plate and glass and headed for the kitchen.

"That was fast," his mother said. His father was in another world.

Theo rinsed his plate and went straight for his backpack on the kitchen counter. A few seconds later he was online, then he opened his mailbox. He clicked on "Urgent Message from GashMail," and saw the photo. Bright, clear, no doubt about who was leaving the police station. His first reaction when reading the description was disbelief. His jaw dropped, his mouth fell open wide, and for several seconds he stared at the image of himself leaving the police station. The shock was quickly replaced by anger. Anger at the lies, the fiction. He had not been arrested. He was not due in court. Then the questions—Who took the photo? Where had they been hiding? Why would anyone tell such outright lies? How many people have seen this? "Guys!" Theo yelled.

His parents crowded behind him and gawked at the monitor sitting on the kitchen counter. A photo taken secretly by some punk and then broadcast to the world with a bunch of lies to describe it. As lawyers, their first reaction was—what could be done legally to stop it, to fix it, to bring the guilty party to justice?

"I'm assuming this is everywhere," Mrs. Boone said.

"Probably so." Theo replied.

"What is GashMail?" Mr. Boone asked.

"It's kind of a shady server you use when you don't want to get caught. A lot of unknown e-mails start there, and it's really hard to track them down."

"So we can't track this?"

"Anything is possible with the Internet, but it would be complicated and expensive."

"The Internet," Mr. Boone said in disgust, and walked to the window above the sink and stared into the darkness of the backyard.

Theo sat down at the table and rubbed his temples. "I guess my life is ruined," he said, and for a moment was near tears.

"This can be explained, Theo," his father said. "Your friends will know the truth. What strangers think doesn't matter."

"That's easy for you to say, Dad. You don't have to face all those kids at school tomorrow. And you don't know how fast rumors fly on the Internet. Half the town is looking at the photo right now and deciding that I'm guilty."

Theo's mother sat next to him and patted his arm. "You're not guilty of anything, Theo, and the truth will come out."

"I'm not so sure about that, Mom. You saw Detective Hamilton today. He thinks I'm guilty. What if they don't find the real thieves? What if they finish their investigation with nothing but me, just me and those three stolen tablets in my locker? At some point, they have to charge somebody with the crime, and it could easily be me. I saw the owner of the store today, they call him Big Mac, and, believe me, he's convinced I'm guilty and he's out for blood. He'll see this photo. The police will see it, too. It makes it easier to believe I'm guilty."

There was a long, heavy pause as Theo's words settled in the kitchen. Was reality gradually seeping in? Was it possible that Theo could actually be charged with the crime? And once the wheels of justice began moving, could the Boones do anything to prevent a terrible outcome?

Each tablet had a value of approximately four hundred dollars, for a total of twelve hundred dollars. When the combined value of stolen goods was in excess of five hundred dollars, then the crime was deemed a felony, a more serious crime than a misdemeanor. Theo knew the law; he'd been pondering it for hours now. He had even double-checked the codes and statutes at the office when he was supposed to be doing his homework. If he were eighteen or older, he would be staring at a felony charge. However, because he was only thirteen, the case would be handled in Juvenile Court where the rules were different. Things were more private there. The files were not made public, nor were the hearings. There were no juries; all matters were decided by a Juvenile Court judge. Jail sentences were rare, and seldom for long periods of time.

If this train wreck continued and Theo somehow got convicted, he could possibly be sentenced to a few months in a detention center for kids.

Jail? Theodore Boone sentenced to serve time?

Outrageous. Crazy. An overreaction. All of the above, but Theo's hyperactive mind was out of control.

His mother was speaking to him. "Theo, the first thing you do is fight back. Attack. When you're right, you never back down. Post a message on your page and tell the truth. E-mail all your friends and tell them this photo and its caption are misleading. Get April, Chase, and Woody and those you trust the most to flood the Internet with the truth. Spread the word that we, your family, are considering legal action."

"We are?" Theo asked.

"Of course we are. We are considering it. It might not work, but we are at least considering it."

"Mom's right, Theo," Mr. Boone said. "The least you can do at this point is put up a fight."

Theo liked it. He had been paralyzed for the past ten minutes, and now it was time for action.

An hour later, the Boones were still at the kitchen table, all three hammering away at their laptops as they tried to chase the rumors while containing them at the same time. It was a losing battle. The photo and its caption were too juicy to ignore, and Theo was proving to be a good target. The only child of two well-known lawyers arrested for breaking and entering, and burglary. Caught red-handed with the stolen goods in his school locker. Like every false rumor, it gained credibility while being repeated, and before long it was practically a fact.

Mr. Boone closed his laptop and began taking notes on his standard yellow pad. At any given moment in Theo's young life, he could walk through the house and lay eyes on at least five yellow legal pads.

"Let's do some detective work," Mr. Boone said. Mrs. Boone removed her reading glasses and closed her laptop, too. She took a sip of herbal tea and said, "Okay, Sherlock Holmes, let's go."

"First, who could break into your locker without being seen?" Mr. Boone asked. "I can't imagine a stranger, an adult, entering the school, going straight to the locker, somehow knowing the code, and breaking in."

"Agreed," said Mrs. Boone. "Theo, do you ever see teachers, or coaches, or janitors or any other adult opening the lockers?"

"Never. You never see them around the lockers. The teachers hang out in the faculty lounge. The janitors have a locker room in the basement, but it's off-limits for students. The coaches use the locker rooms at the gym."

"So an adult would be noticed?"

Theo thought for a moment, then said, "If we knew the adult, and she was opening one of our lockers, then, sure, we would make a note of it. That would be unusual. If it were a stranger, we would probably say something to the person. I don't know for sure because it's never happened."

"But this is between classes when the halls are busy, right?" asked Mr. Boone.

"Yes."

"What about while you're in class and the halls are empty?"

Theo thought some more. "The halls are rarely empty. During class there's usually someone going somewhere—a student with a hall pass, a janitor, a teacher's assistant."

"What about security cameras in the halls?" Mr. Boone asked.

"They took them down a few weeks ago to install a new system."

Mrs. Boone said, "Sounds to me like it would be too risky for an adult to open a student's locker."

"I agree," Theo said. "But every crime has some risk, right?"

"Sure, but isn't the risk much greater for someone who does not normally use a locker?"

"Yes," Mr. Boone said with certainty. "And even riskier for someone from outside the school. I say we eliminate that person. Can we agree that this is an inside job, someone from inside the school?"

Theo shrugged but did not disagree, nor did his mother.

Mr. Boone continued, "Someone who knows how to open the locker. Someone who could steal the code. And, someone with easy access to the bike racks where it takes about two seconds to poke a hole in a tire. Someone who knows Theo's bike, knows where he parks it. Someone who knows his schedule and movements. Someone who knows Theo well and can watch him without getting caught."

"Another student?" Theo asked.

"Exactly."

Mrs. Boone was skeptical. "I find it hard to believe that a thirteen-year-old could break into the computer store, avoid the security cameras, and make a clean getaway."

"That's more believable than a janitor or a teacher's assistant," Mr. Boone replied.

There was a long pause as the three detectives took a deep breath and considered this. Theo spoke first. "He had a partner, right? Remember the anonymous call from the pay phone near the hospital. Plus, it would take at least two people to haul away all the stolen goods from the computer store."

"Exactly," Mr. Boone said again. "And look at the technical know-how involved here. Someone hacked into the school's file and got the code. Someone was clever enough to snap a photo of us this afternoon as we left the police station, and knew how to use this GashMail to distribute it without getting caught. Sounds like a kid to me."

"I guess anyone could throw a rock through a window," Mrs. Boone observed.

"Yes, but it does seem more of a juvenile act, doesn't it?"

All three agreed.

Theo said, "And I guess most kids in the school, at least most of the boys, know when and where the Boy Scouts meet. It wouldn't be difficult to sneak around the VFW and find my bike during the meeting."

The evidence was becoming overwhelming.

"How many students are in the middle school, Theo?" Mrs. Boone asked.

"Five sections in grades five through eight. That's about eighty for each grade, times four, so somewhere around three hundred and twenty."

"Let's eliminate the girls," Mr. Boone said. "I can't see a girl slashing tires or throwing rocks through windows."

"I don't know, Dad. We have some pretty rough girls in our school."

"Humor me for now, Theo. We can talk about the girls later."

"Okay, now we're down to a hundred and sixty boys," Theo said. "Where do we start?"

The trail suddenly seemed a bit cooler. Mr. and Mrs. Boone knew Theo was a popular kid who did not bully or fight or start trouble.

Mr. Boone said, "We know your friends, Theo, but that's only a handful. We don't know the majority of the students at school. Why don't you make a list of possible suspects? Kids you've had disagreements with. Kids who may carry a grudge for something that happened recently, or a year ago."

"What about the Debate Team?" Mrs. Boone asked. "You've never lost a debate. Maybe someone on the losing side got their feelings hurt."

"Maybe one of your fellow Scouts is jealous," added Mr. Boone.

Theo was nodding along, his mind racing and trying to imagine possible enemies. He said, "Well, I'm sure there are kids who don't like me, but why this? It seems like they're going overboard to settle a grudge, a grudge I know nothing about."

"Indeed it does," said Mrs. Boone.

"Think about it, Theo. Make a list of your top suspects, and we'll discuss them over dinner tomorrow night."

"I'll try," Theo said.

Chapter II

Thursday morning. Theo was wide awake when his alarm rang at 7:30. There was a knot in his stomach, and he was certain he was too sick to go to school. He stared at the ceiling and waited for his illness to grow worse, to hopefully become a full-blown bout of nausea that would make him heave and vomit. His head hurt, too, and he was convinced a migraine was on its way, though he had never had one. Minutes passed, unfortunately his condition did not deteriorate.

How could he walk into school and face all the suspicion? How could he survive the jokes and snide comments and teasing? If there had ever been a perfect day to skip school, play hooky, call in sick, whatever, then it was today.

Judge moved first. He popped up from under the bed and was ready to go. Theo envied him. His day would be spent at the office, sleeping next to Elsa's desk, roaming from one room to the next, hanging out in the kitchen looking for food, and napping in Theo's office, waiting for him to arrive from school. No worries, no stress, no fears of someone stalking him and plotting more mischief. What a life, thought Theo. A dog's life. It didn't seem fair.

Theo sat on the edge of his bed, waited for a moment in hopes he would throw up, but soon admitted that he was feeling better. Judge just stared at him. There were footsteps outside his door, then a gentle knock. "Theo," his mother said softly. "Are you awake?"

"Yes, ma'am," Theo said in a fake scratchy voice, as if he might be taking his last breath.

She opened the door, stepped inside, and sat next to him on the bed. "Here, I brought you a cup of hot chocolate." Theo took the cup and held it with both hands. The aroma was strong and delicious.

"Did you sleep well?" she asked. She was still in her heavy bathrobe and her favorite pink fuzzy slippers.

"Not really," Theo said. "I had this nightmare that wouldn't go away."

"Tell me about it," she said as she tussled his hair.

Theo took a sip of the hot chocolate and smacked

his lips. "It was a really weird dream that made no sense at all, and it seemed to go on and on. I was running from the police, lots of police, with guns and everything. I was on my bike, getting away, leaving them behind, when they shot out both tires. So I threw the bike in a ditch and ran through the woods. They were getting closer and closer, bullets hitting trees all around me, and they had dogs, too, and the dogs were right on my heels. Someone yelled, 'Hey, Theo, over here.' I ran to the voice and it was Pete Duffy, in a pickup truck. So I jumped in the back of the truck and we took off, bullets still flying all around us. He was driving like a maniac, slinging me all over the back of the truck, and suddenly we were on Main Street and people were yelling, 'Go, Theo, Go' and stuff like that. Police cars were behind us with lights and sirens. We smashed through a roadblock and were about to get away when the cops shot out all four tires."

Theo paused, took another sip. Judge was staring at him with only one thought—where's breakfast?

"Did you get away?" his mom asked. She seemed to be amused by the story.

"I'm not sure. I don't think I finished the dream. We were running through some alleys, and every time we turned a corner there were more policemen, all of them blasting away. It was like a small army was after us. There was a SWAT team, and even a helicopter overhead. Pete Duffy kept saying, 'They're not going to catch us, Theo. Just keep running.' We ran through the courthouse, which was full of people, in the middle of the night, and we ran toward the river. For some reason we decided to cross the bridge. About halfway over, we saw a SWAT team on the other side, coming right at us. We stopped, looked behind, saw cops and dogs everywhere. Pete Duffy said, 'We gotta jump, Theo.' And I said, 'I'm not jumping.' So he crawled over the railing and was about to jump when he got hit with bullets from all sides. He screamed and fell over, and I watched him fall until he hit the water. There were people on the river in boats, and they cheered when he made a splash. Then they started yelling, 'Jump, Theo, Jump!' The police were closing in from both sides. The dogs were growling, sirens blaring away, gunfire. I held up my hands like I was going to surrender, then in a split second I jumped over the railing—which was about eight feet high—but this was a dream, okay? I looked like an Olympic diver flying through the air. On the way down I started doing flips and twists and turns, don't know where I learned all those moves. The river was far below and getting closer and closer."

He took another sip.

"What happened?" she asked.

"Don't know. That dive lasted for a long time, and I woke up before I hit the water. I tried to go back to sleep to finish the dive but couldn't get it to work."

"That's a pretty cool dream, Theo. Lots of action and excitement."

"It wasn't very cool at the time. I was scared to death. You ever been shot at by the police?"

"No, I have not. You were going to think about some possible enemies who might be carrying a grudge of some sort."

Theo took another sip and thought for a moment. "Come on, Mom. Kids don't have enemies, do they? Look, we all have people we don't like, and don't like us, right? But I can't think of a single person I'd call an enemy."

"Fair enough. Who is the kid who dislikes you the most?"

"Betty Ann Hockner."

"And what's the history?"

"We had a debate several months ago, boys versus girls. The issue was gun control. Things got pretty heated, but it was all fair. We won the debate and she was really upset. I heard later that she called me a 'jerk' and a 'cheap-shot artist.' I've seen her almost every day since then, and she gives me these looks like she would love to slit my throat."

"You should reach out to her, Theo."

"No way."

"And why not?"

"I'm afraid she'll slit my throat."

"Could she slash your tires and throw a rock through a window?"

Theo shook his head and thought for a second. "Not really. She's a nice girl, but she's not very popular. I kinda feel sorry for her. She's not our suspect."

"So who is?"

"I don't know. I'm still thinking about it."

"You'd better get ready for school."

"I feel pretty lousy, Mom, nausea and a headache. I think I'd better stay in bed today."

She smiled, tussled his hair again, didn't believe a word of it, and said, "What a surprise. You know, Theo, if you didn't fake so many illnesses in order to skip school, I might believe you every now and then."

"School's boring."

"Well, it's not optional. If you want to go to law school, there is a rule somewhere that you must complete the eighth grade."

"Show me that rule."

"I just made it up. Look, Theo, today might be a bit rough. Lots of gossip and such, and probably some jokes. I know you'd rather skip it, but you can't. Bite your lip, grit your teeth, and hold your head up because you've done nothing wrong. You have nothing to be ashamed of."

"I know."

"And keep smiling. The world is a brighter place when you're smiling."

"It might be hard to smile today."

Theo parked his bike at a different rack, one by the cafeteria, and after he chained it he couldn't help but look around to see if anyone was watching. This looking over his shoulder was already a habit, and he was tired of it.

It was 8:20. He met April Finnemore in the cafeteria where students who arrive early on buses were allowed to meet and socialize, or have an apple juice, or to sometimes study. April was a friend, a close one, but not a girlfriend. Theo trusted her above all others, and she confided in him as well. Her home life was a constant mess, with a father who came and went, a mother who was at least half crazy if not more, and older siblings who had already fled town. April, too, wanted to leave home but was much too young. Her dream was to be an artist and live in Paris.

"How are you doing?" she asked as they sat at the end of a long table, as far away from the other students as possible.

Theo gritted his teeth, held up his head, and said, "I'm fine. Nothing wrong with me."

"This stuff is all over the Internet. It seems to be growing."

"Look, April, I can't control that. I'm innocent. What am I supposed to do about it? You want an apple juice?"

"Sure."

Theo walked across the cafeteria to a counter where cups of free apple juice were waiting. He picked up two, and was walking back to April when a group of seventh-grade boys began chanting, "Guilty! Guilty! Guilty!"

Theo looked at them and flashed his braces, offered a fake smile, as if he found it humorous. The biggest loudmouth was a kid named Phil Jacoby, a tough kid from a bad part of town. Theo knew him but they did not hang out. A few other kids joined in, "Guilty! Guilty! Guilty!" But by the time Theo sat down the chants were dying; the fun was over.

"Creeps," April hissed as she glared at the boys.

"Just ignore them," Theo said. "If you fight back, it just gets worse."

More kids arrived and backpacks hit the tables.

"What will the police do next?" April asked, almost in a whisper.

"Finish their investigation," Theo said softly, glancing around. "There are no fingerprints on the tablets found in my locker, so they figure the thief is pretty smart. They were going to dust my locker, but now they figure that's a waste of time. You gotta keep in mind, April, this is a minor crime. The cops have much more important matters to worry about."

"Like finding Pete Duffy."

"Exactly. Plus they have drug cases and more serious crimes to investigate. They won't spend a lot of time on this burglary. It's not that serious."

"Unless you're the accused. Don't tell me you're not worried about getting framed for this."

"Sure, I'm worried, but I trust the police and the courts. You gotta trust the system, April. I'm innocent and I know it. The police will find the real thieves and I'll be off the hook."

"Just that simple?"

"Yes. I think."

The gang of seventh graders walked behind him. Phil Jacoby said loudly, "Hey, you guys, watch your backpacks. Theo the Thief is in the room." His buddies howled with laughter but kept walking. The other students glared at Theo. A couple moved their backpacks closer.

"Oh boy," Theo said, defeated. "I guess I have a new nickname."

"Creeps."

Theo found it difficult to bite his lip, grit his teeth, and hold up his head. This would indeed be a long day.

The fight broke out a few minutes later as Theo was closing his locker. The troublemaker was another loudmouth, a kid named Baxter who was in Madame Monique's eighth-grade homeroom and had a locker not far from Theo's. Baxter walked behind Theo, and in a loud voice, said, "Hey, what's up, jailbird?" This got a few laughs but not nearly as many as Baxter was looking for. He stopped and grinned at Theo.

Baxter's mistake was opening his big mouth when Woody happened to be closing his own locker. He whirled around and angrily said, "Shut up!"

Nobody messed with Woody. He had two older brothers who played football and loved karate and were known to fight for any reason. Woody's home was in a constant state of physical conflict, with broken windows, furniture, and sometimes bones. As the youngest, Woody had been the tackling dummy and the punching bag, and he actually enjoyed a good fight with someone his own size. He was never a bully, but often he was too quick to throw a punch, or to threaten a classmate.

But Baxter had his own tough-guy reputation, and he could not back down with people watching. "Don't tell me to shut up," he shot back. "If I want to call Theo a jailbird, then I'll call him a jailbird."

Woody was already walking toward Baxter, and at that point serious trouble was inevitable. Excitement gripped the hallway as the other students realized that, like a couple of gunslingers, neither of these two would back down.

Theo glanced up and down the hall in hopes of seeing Mr. Mount or another teacher, but there was no adult in sight at that crucial moment. He said, "It's okay, Woody, it's okay."

But it wasn't okay with Woody. He glared at Baxter and said, "Take it back."

Baxter said, "No, thanks. When you steal and get arrested, then in my book you're a jailbird." He was still talking tough, but his eyes were also getting bigger. His left eye, though, was about to get closed.

Woody lunged with a right hook that landed perfectly on Baxter's face. Baxter, to his credit, managed to land a solid punch before both boys locked each other up in death grips and tumbled to the floor. Fights were rare at the middle school and a good one was not to be missed. A crowd gathered around instantly. Down the hall someone yelled, "A fight! A fight!" Woody and Baxter were sliding all over the tiled floor, clawing and scratching like two cats.

Baxter's sidekick was a runt named Griff, and evidently he knew what the other boys knew—it would only be a matter of seconds before Woody gained the upper hand and began working on Baxter's face. So Griff, to protect his friend, made the dumb move of joining the fray. He growled some sort of impromptu battle cry and lunged himself onto Woody's back. Theo and the rest of the crowd gawked in disbelief.

Fighting carried an automatic suspension from classes. The student manual was clear and every teacher stressed the evils of fighting. The punishment, handed down by Mrs. Gladwell, was flexible and depended on the circumstances. A push-and-shove match on the playground might result in a one-day suspension with three extra hours in study hall. A full-blown fist fight with busted lips and bloody noses might result in a three-day suspension, no after-school activities, and one month of probation.

Theo was not a fighter. His last scuffle had been in fourth grade when he and Walter Norris got in a heated wrestling match at the city swimming pool. But as he stood there, frozen, and watched the fight right in front of him, he suddenly had the urge to join it. After all, his friend Woody was slugging it out in defense of his honor. The least Theo could do was go to his rescue. And perhaps a suspension was not the end of the world. His parents would go berserk, but they would eventually settle down. What did his mother say last night? "The first thing you do is fight back. Attack. When you're right, you never back down."

Ike would be proud.

Sometimes, a guy has got to fight.

Theo dropped his backpack, yelled something that not even he understood, and jumped into the pile.

Chapter 12

On one side of the table, Baxter sat with Griff, and on the other side Woody sat with Theo. The opposing sides faced each other as the tension slowly faded and reality set in. Baxter had an ice pack on the side of his face and his left eye was swollen and completely closed. It looked awful. Woody was proud, though he suppressed a smile. With suspension coming and angry parents to deal with, smiles were not possible. Griff's face showed no damage, nor did Woody's. Theo's bottom lip was puffy and there was a spot of dried blood on it. He tapped it with a tissue. His more serious wound was a throbbing head, courtesy of a kick at the bottom of the pile by either Baxter or Griff, but he did not mention this.

Mr. Mount sat at the end of the table and stared at the boys. He had angrily pulled them apart and marched them down to the library and into the small study room where they were now sitting and cooling off. As the seconds and minutes ticked by, the boys settled down. Their breathing slowed. Their heart rates were returning to normal. Nothing like a good fight to get the pulse racing and the blood pumping.

"What happened?" Mr. Mount finally asked.

All four boys stared at the table. Nothing. Not a word.

"Could this have anything to do with the rumor that Theo was arrested yesterday?" Mr. Mount asked, looking squarely at Theo, who did not take his eyes off the surface of the table.

Mr. Mount knew that Woody was a hothead and Baxter liked trouble. He also knew that Griff followed Baxter around like a new puppy. He would never believe, though, that Theo Boone would start a fight, or jump into the middle of one. But Mr. Mount had once been a boy, and he understood things. The way he figured it, Baxter and Griff were picking on Theo, and Woody defended his friend.

There were voices outside the room. Mr. Mount said, "I think Mrs. Gladwell is here. I wouldn't want to be in your shoes." With that, he stood and left the room. As soon as the door closed behind him, Woody snarled, "Nobody rats, okay? I mean it, nobody rats. Not one word."

As soon as the words left his mouth, the door opened wide and Mrs. Gladwell stormed in. One look, and the boys knew they were dead.

She stared at them as she slowly took a seat at the end of the table. Mr. Mount eased into the room, closed the door, and stood against the wall. He was there as her witness.

"Are you okay, Baxter?" she asked, without a touch of sympathy.

Baxter nodded slightly.

"And Theo? Is that blood on your bottom lip?"

Theo nodded slightly.

She stiffened her spine, frowned even harder, and began, "Well, I want to know what happened."

Neither boy moved the tiniest muscle. All seven eyes (Baxter had only one workable eye at this point) were glued firmly at something fascinating, though invisible, on the table. Silence, as seconds passed. Her face became redder, her frown even harsher.

"Fighting is a very serious offense," she lectured. "We do not tolerate fighting at this school, and you've known this since you arrived here in the fifth grade. Fighting carries an automatic suspension. A suspension goes into your file and becomes part of your permanent record."

Not exactly, Theo said to himself. Sure, it might be a permanent record, but it would never leave the middle school. No college or law school or potential employer would ever know that a student got suspended for fighting in the eighth grade.

"Theo," she said sternly, "I want to know what happened. Look at me, Theo."

Theo slowly turned and looked at the rather frightening face of his principal. "Tell me what happened," she demanded. Theo, unable to maintain eye contact, focused his attention at a spot on the wall and clenched his jaws.

Of the four, Theo was a leader; Griff was a follower; Woody and Baxter generally moved with the pack. If Theo kept his mouth shut, then the other three would, too. This was Mrs. Gladwell's first mistake.

The way to crack a case with multiple defendants is to separate them. Theo, if in charge, would isolate Griff in a small room with several grim-faced adults—administrators, coaches, people with clout and authority. They would explain to Griff that the other three boys were talking and pointing the finger at him. "Griff, Baxter is saying that you were taunting Theo." And, "Griff, they're saying you threw the first punch." And so on. Griff wouldn't believe this at first, but after a few minutes of getting hammered at, he would eventually start talking. Once he gave his version, he would be told that it didn't jive with the other three; so, obviously, Griff was lying. Lying would only compound his troubles. Lying, plus fighting, would lead to an even longer suspension and probation. Griff would then become desperate to make it known that his version was indeed truthful and accurate. Once this strategy was used on all four boys, they would be singing like birds and the truth about the fight would become clear.

This, of course, would require deception on the part of the authorities, but such tactics are permissible under the law. On the other hand, Mrs. Gladwell's strategy involved no deception, and she would learn nothing from the boys. Theo was happy that she did not understand basic police interrogation tactics.

Theo said nothing and returned his gaze to the table in front of him. His refusal to speak, to rat, meant all four would go down together.

She continued, "Baxter, who punched you in the eye?"

Baxter lowered the ice pack and set it on the table. The ice was working and the swelling had gone down a little. He almost said, "I don't know," but caught himself. He, of course, did know. There was no benefit in lying at this point. Just clam up like Theo and suffer through this.

There was a long pause as she waited. The air was thick with tension and looming trouble. None of the boys had ever been suspended, though Woody and Baxter had been on probation a couple of times.

Mrs. Gladwell had been informed early that morning the Internet was buzzing with the rumors that Theo had been arrested for the theft and was going to court. She had been shown the photo posted on GashMail. She had planned to meet with Theo at some point during the day and offer her support. Now, she was faced with the unpleasant task of suspending him and the other three.

. Finally, she said, "I suspect that either Baxter or Griff said something about Theo getting into trouble with the law, maybe getting arrested or something like that. Since Woody and Theo are classmates and good friends, I suspect that Woody intervened and this started the fight. Am I right about this, Griff?"

Griff jerked as though he'd been slapped, but he quickly composed himself so he could say nothing. Not a word. He narrowed his eyes and gritted his teeth and gave her nothing.

She waited and waited and her frown disappeared. The boys were playing games, so she would play along. "Baxter?"

Baxter tapped the table nervously but said nothing.

"Boys, we can sit here all morning," she said.

Behind her, Mr. Mount tried not to smile. Secretly, he

admired the boys for protecting each other and facing their punishment together.

"Mr. Mount, would you take Baxter, Griff, and Woody outside?" she said. "I want to talk to Theo alone." Without a word, the three followed Mr. Mount out of the room. When the door closed, Theo felt totally isolated.

"Look at me, Theo," she said softly. Theo turned and made eye contact.

"I know you've had a bad week," she said. "You feel as though you're the victim. The police are after you. Someone is trying to frame you for the burglary. Someone is stalking you. Someone is bullying you. Your face is all over the Internet in that photo of you and your parents leaving the police station. Lies are being told. Rumors are out of control. I understand all this, Theo. I'm on your side, and I hope you know this."

Theo managed to nod slightly.

"And I'm certain that you did not start this fight. I want you to tell me exactly what happened, okay?"

"I got in a fight," Theo said.

"But did you start the fight, Theo?"

"I got in a fight and fighting is against the rules." He found the strong urge to look away, but somehow managed to stare at her. She was disappointed, even hurt, and Theo felt lousy. He considered her a friend, an ally, a person of authority who was trying to help him, and he was giving her nothing.

After a long, tense, nervous, silent pause, she said, "So, you're not going to tell me what happened?"

Theo shook his head. It hurt more when he moved it.

Then a cruel question: "What will your parents think when I call them and tell them you've been suspended from school for fighting?"

"I don't know," Theo managed to say, horrified by the prospect. Facing his parents would be far worse than getting kicked in the head. A sharp pain stabbed him in the stomach as he saw the looks in their eyes.

"Okay, please step outside."

Theo quickly jumped from his chair and left the room. When he stepped through the door, he saw the other three and ran his index finger across his mouth. Lips are zipped. I didn't rat, and you don't either.

Baxter was next. He returned to the room, to the table, as if he might be executed.

"Did you say something to Theo about getting into trouble?" she asked.

No response.

"Did you taunt him or harass him?"

No response.

"Did Woody hit you in the face?"

No response.

"Did Theo?"

Nothing.

"Would you please step outside and send in Woody," she said.

When Baxter stepped through the door and saw the other three, he ran his index finger across his lips. Nobody rats.

While Woody was getting grilled by Mrs. Gladwell, Theo and Griff and Baxter sat on a wooden bench under the watch of Mr. Mount, who felt sorry for the boys. They were all good kids and nothing would be gained by suspensions. Still, rules were rules.

Of the four, Woody would be the last to crack under pressure, and he refused to answer any question from Mrs. Gladwell. When she asked him if he hit Baxter, he responded, "Name, rank, and serial number only."

"Very funny, Woody. You think this is a game?"

"No."

"Did you throw the first punch?"

"I refuse to incriminate myself," he replied.

"Get out of here."

The weakest link was Griff, and when he survived his little question-and-answer period with Mrs. Gladwell by refusing to rat, she reassembled the four boys in the room. She said, "Very well. I'm going to suspend each of you one day for fighting, and another day for your refusal to cooperate. Today is Thursday and the suspension will run today and tomorrow. You will return to classes on Monday, at which time you will begin a thirty-day probation. Any violation during the next thirty days, and you will be suspended for a week."

The prospect of missing classes for two days did not really trouble Theo, but the reality of facing his parents was painful. He thought about calling Ike first because Ike would understand and probably praise Theo for taking a stand. Perhaps Ike could then break the news to Theo's parents and soften the impact. Theo was contemplating this when Mrs. Gladwell said, "I'll call your parents."

It took an hour to work out the details of the suspensions and do the paperwork. The boys stayed in the room, at the table, facing each other while Mr. Mount sat, bored, at the end of the table. He stepped out once to get coffee, and while he was gone Baxter said, "Sorry, Theo."

"No problem," Theo said.

Woody did not apologize.

Woody's parents and Baxter's parents had jobs; thus,

no one was home during the day. Mrs. Gladwell explained they would be receiving "in-school suspensions" and would be required to sit in separate study rooms at school from 8:40 a.m. until classes ended at 3:30. They would be alone with nothing to do but extra homework. No cell phones, laptops, nothing but textbooks. They would eat lunch at their desks, alone. This seemed far worse than the old-fashioned suspensions where they kicked you off campus. Griff's mother was a housewife so he could stay at home, and probably sleep late, watch television, play with the dog, and do whatever he wanted, unless, of course, his parents were ticked off enough to impose penalties. Theo, too, had a place to go—the offices of Boone & Boone.

His mother was in court. His father picked him up from school. As they were driving away, Theo said, "What about my bike?"

"We'll get it later," his father replied. So far, he had been remarkably cool and undisturbed, at least on the surface.

A block or two later, his father said, "What happened?"

"It's just between me and you, right?"

"What happened, Theo!" his father snapped.

"You're not telling Mrs. Gladwell, are you? I can't rat on the other guys."

"No. Just tell me what happened."

Theo told him everything. The details poured forth in a rush, and Theo, who had been unable to tell his side of the story, unloaded. When he finished they were sitting in the small parking lot behind the office. "Are you upset with me, Dad?" Theo asked.

"You know the rules, and you broke the rules," Mr. Boone said sternly.

"I did, but at the time, I had no choice."

Mr. Boone turned off the ignition and said, "That's the way I see it, too."

Chapter 13

Theo sat in his dark office, lights off, shades pulled, just him and Judge brooding in the shadows and thinking about what could possibly happen next. In a couple of hours, his mother would return from court. She and his father would huddle behind a locked door and have one of those deadly serious conversations that only troubled parents can have. Then he would be hauled in like a felon to face the music. He would be lectured. His mother would cry. Suspended from school! How could he do such a thing? And on and on. He was already tired of thinking about it.

His father's initial response was somewhat comforting. There had been no drama, though his father generally was not one for theatrics. No yelling, but then Woods Boone was too laid back to yell. No threats or additional punishment, though Theo knew his parents always chatted first before throwing the book at him.

Until a few hours earlier, Theo had never dreamed he would get suspended from school. He had never thought about it, and as he pondered the incident he asked himself if it was worth it. He didn't believe in breaking rules. He didn't enjoy disappointing Mrs. Gladwell and Mr. Mount. He suspected his parents would view it as an embarrassment, and this troubled him. And, to be honest, there had been no pleasure in the violence, the frantic melee in which all four warriors seemed to be kicking, punching, scratching, and cursing each other while some students in the crowd gawked in awe and others egged them on.

On the other hand, there was some pride in the fact that he had gone to the aid of a friend who was being double-teamed. He had seen the admiration in the eyes of the spectators, his classmates and friends. He, Theo Boone, was being falsely accused, and had gone on the attack to defend his good name and also to protect a friend.

What a friend! Theo could not help but smile as he replayed the encounter. He marveled at the speed and fearlessness with which Woody had stepped forward and shut up big-mouth Baxter. And, Theo had a hunch Woody was not finished. Most likely, he would wait until he caught

Baxter off-campus and close his other eye. Theo hoped his fighting days were over, but if another bout popped up he wanted Woody nearby.

There was a soft knock on the door. "Come in," Theo said.

It was Elsa, red-eyed and with tears on her cheeks. She flipped the light switch and reached down to hug him. "Theo, I'm so sorry," she said.

"It's okay, it's okay," he said. This was the last thing he wanted—big-time drama from those who loved him. He endured the hug. "I'm fine. It's nothing, okay?" he said, getting irritated. She stood and wiped her cheeks with a tissue. "I can't believe it. You're the nicest kid in the world."

"Probably not. Maybe top five. Look, Elsa, I'm okay."

"Who attacked you?"

"No one. It was just a stupid fight, okay? No big deal."

She patted her cheeks with the tissue and began to realize that her sympathies were not being appreciated. "I still love you, Theo," she said, as if he had killed someone.

"I'm fine, Elsa, just fine." Now would you please get out of here?

She left and Theo turned off the light. He and Judge returned to their brooding, which was actually quite enjoyable. Five minutes passed and there was another knock at the door. "Yes," he said. The door opened slowly and Dorothy, his father's real estate secretary, took a step inside. She flipped on the light and said, "Theo, are you okay?"

"Yes," he said, shortly, and for a long second he was afraid she might lunge at him with an awkward hug, as if he needed her physical support.

"I can't believe it. Why would the school suspend you?"

"Because I got in a fight, plain and simple. Fighting is against the rules."

"Yes, but, Theo, surely it wasn't your fault."

Theo shook his head and looked out the window. How many times would he be forced to explain what happened? "Doesn't matter who's at fault. A fight is a fight."

After an awkward pause, she said, "Well, if you need a friend, I'm just down the hall."

"Thanks." Oh sure. I'm going to unload my troubles to a fully grown adult who's old enough to be my mother.

She left and Theo turned off the light. His cell phone beeped with a text from April Finnemore.

Just heard. U ok?
   Yep. At office. No classes. Luv it.
Your parents?
   Mom n court. Dad's not 2 sore.
Who'd u punch?

Not sure. Lot of contact.
Wounds? Blood?

Theo suddenly wished he had more to show for his efforts. Typically, he decided to exaggerate a little. He wrote:

Busted lip. Blood.
Awesome! When can I see?
Later. U need to study now.

He again returned to his brooding. Five minutes later, there was a knock at the door. Before Theo could respond, Vince stepped in and turned on the light. With his arrival, the entire firm of Boone & Boone had now come to pay its respects. Except, of course, Marcella Boone, who would arrive soon enough.

Vince had been her paralegal for many years. He did the grunt work for Mrs. Boone's divorce cases, and it was not always pleasant. He spent a lot of time out of the office, investigating clients, and spying on their husbands, and checking facts. Theo had known for many years that divorce clients often do not tell the truth to their lawyers, and Vince was called upon to verify their stories. He was about thirty-five, single, a nice guy with a tough job.

Elsa had entered the room crying. Dorothy seemed

ready for a breakdown. But not Vince. He was smiling as he leaned against the door. "Way to go, Theo. Did you pop him a good one?"

Theo smiled, finally. He realized he would tell his story a hundred times, so why not dress it up a bit? "Yep," he said.

"Attaboy. Look, Theo, you've just learned a valuable lesson. There comes a time when you gotta stand your ground, regardless of the circumstances."

"I couldn't back down," Theo said.

"Suspensions are no big deal, as long as they don't become a habit. I got one in the sixth grade."

"No kidding?"

"True story. I grew up in Northchester and we walked to school. There was a bully named Jerry Prater, a tough kid, and he was giving me a hard time. About once a week, he would catch me on the playground before school and knock me down, kick me some, and grab my lunch box. He would take the good stuff, the chips, Twinkies, ham sandwiches, and leave me the apples and carrots. The next day, he would grab one of my buddies and go through the same routine. I guess Jerry was always hungry. Anyway, he was making our lives pretty miserable. I had an older brother in high school, and he explained to me that bullies are really cowards and until you take a stand things will just get worse. My brother told me what to do. I hid my lunch in my backpack and filled my lunch box with rocks. The next morning I saw Jerry on the playground and headed toward him. He was about to punch me when I suddenly swung the lunch box and hit him in the face. Hard. I mean it was a nasty blow that cut a gash in his cheekbone. He screamed and fell down, and I whacked him a few more times in the head. There was a crowd by now, and a teacher came running over. They took him to the doctor and sewed him up. Eighteen stitches, ten across his cheekbone. Everybody yelled at me and my dad came to the school and picked me up. I explained the situation and he had no problem with it. My mom cried, but that's what moms do. Anyway, Jerry left me alone after that."

"That's awesome. How long was the suspension?"

"A week. I was a hero for a short time, but after a while I felt bad about it. Jerry Prater deserved to get punched, but he had this scar on his face. That was my last fight, Theo. I stood up to a bully, but I used a weapon. I should have used my fists and nothing else. I still feel bad about it."

"What happened to Jerry?"

"He dropped out of school and later went to prison. Never had much of a chance. Anyway, you did the right thing, so don't spend too much time worrying about it."

"I don't want my mom to yell at me."

"She won't. I know that woman very well, Theo."

After he left, Theo fell asleep and Judge went to look for food.

They met in the conference room during lunch. Theo sat at the end of the long, imposing table, with a parent on each side. Before him was a chicken salad sandwich which he had no desire to eat. His appetite was gone.

His mother was not smiling but she wasn't yelling either. It was obvious that she and Mr. Boone had had their little private meeting about their son and his suspension, so Mrs. Boone was over the shock.

"If this happened again, what would you do differently, Theo?" she asked, calmly, as she sipped an iced tea.

Theo chewed on a piece of lettuce and considered the question, which he found interesting. "Well, Mom, I'm not sure. I could do nothing to prevent the fight because it began so quickly. And, I couldn't exactly break it up because Woody and Baxter were really going at it. When Griff jumped on Woody, I felt like I had no choice. Woody was fighting for me. The least I could do was help him."

"So, you wouldn't do anything differently?"

"I guess not."

"Does that mean you've learned nothing from this little episode?"

"I've learned that I don't like fighting. Getting punched in the face and kicked in the head is not that pleasant. There are a few guys who like to fight, but not me."

"I'd say that is a valuable lesson learned," Mr. Boone chimed in as he took a bite of his sandwich.

It appeared as though Mrs. Boone was about to begin a lecture when Elsa tapped on the door. She opened it and said, "Sorry to bother, but the police are here."

"Why?" Mr. Boone asked. Theo wanted to crawl under the table.

"They want to talk to Theo, and his parents, of course."

Detectives Hamilton and Vorman were back. With lunch interrupted, they settled into two seats on one side of the table and placed a large white envelope in front of them. The Boones readjusted themselves on the other side.

"Sorry to disturb lunch," Hamilton said. "We stopped by to chat with the two of you and were told that Theo is here. A suspension?"

"That's correct," Mrs. Boone said sharply. She was obviously irritated.

"Suspension for what?"

"I'll be happy to answer that if you can convince me it's any of your business."

It was none of their business, and Hamilton's face blushed as his partner gave him a look of frustration.

Go get 'em, Mom, Theo said to himself. With a lawyer on each side, he felt well protected. However, he was nervous and sitting on his hands to keep them from shaking.

"I'm sure there's a good reason for this visit," Mr. Boone said.

Vorman leaned forward and said, "Yes, well, we wanted to talk to Theo about the baseball cap that was stolen from his locker on Monday. Would you describe it for us, Theo?"

Theo looked up at his mother, then at his father. Both nodded. Go ahead, answer the question. He said, "It's navy blue with a red bill, adjustable strap, with the Twins logo in the middle of the front."

"Any idea who made the cap?" Vorman asked.

"Nike."

"Any identifying marks on the cap?"

"My initials, T.B., on the underside of the bill."

"What did you use to write your initials?"

"A black Magic Marker."

Vorman slowly opened the envelope, removed a cap, and slid it across the table to Theo. "Is this your cap?"

Theo held it, gave it a quick inspection, and said, "Yes, sir."

"Where did you find it?" Mrs. Boone asked.

"At the computer store, Big Mac's. The cleaning crew comes in every Wednesday night, after hours. Last night, they were doing the floors when one of them swept under a counter and found this. The thief broke in around nine p.m. Tuesday night, and somehow in the mad scramble to steal what he wanted and make a quick getaway, he lost his cap."

Theo stared at the cap and wanted to cry. His favorite cap was now being used as evidence against him. It did not seem fair. The proof was piling up. For some weird reason he could hear Baxter's obnoxious voice: "Jailbird. Jailbird."

For a moment, his parents seemed unable to speak. Theo wasn't about to make a sound. The detectives stared at them with looks of grim satisfaction, as if to say, "You're nailed. Let's see you worm your way out of it this time."

Finally, Mrs. Boone cleared her throat and said, "Looks as though the thief is very clever. He planned his crime carefully, with the intention of framing Theo. On Monday, he stole the cap, then left it at the scene of the crime, and on Wednesday he returned to the locker with the stolen goods."

"That's one theory," Vorman said, "And you might be right. But we're also working with another theory, one that has Theo wearing the cap Tuesday night, maybe to help disguise his face when he entered the store, around nine, and we know he was in the vicinity around that time, he even admits this, and in his rush to grab the tablets and laptops and cell phones he lost his cap, and here it is. And, of course, we found some of the stolen loot in his locker on Wednesday."

"It's kinda hard to ignore Theo as a suspect," Hamilton added.

"Very hard," Vorman agreed. "In fact, with most investigations we don't have this much evidence against a suspect."

It was Hamilton's turn. "We find it odd that you didn't report the first break-in on Monday. Locker theft is rare at the school, yet you didn't report it. And you have given us no good reason for this failure."

Vorman: "It could be that there was no break-in on Monday. When you got caught with the stolen tablets on Wednesday, you said someone broke in and left them in your locker. To make this sound believable, you added the little twist that someone had robbed your locker two days before."

Hamilton: "But there was no record of that. No proof."

Vorman: "And this mysterious thief was unseen by anyone at the school. Kinda hard to believe with eighty eighth graders and dozens of teachers, plus janitors and assistants. Busy hallways and such. Hard to believe."

Hamilton: "Pretty incredible story, if you ask me."

This tag team was making Theo sick. He closed his eyes, gritted his teeth, and told himself not to cry.

"You don't believe my son?" Mrs. Boone asked. To Theo, it was obvious that they did not.

"Let's just say that we're still investigating," Vorman replied.

"Did you check the cap for fingerprints?" Mr. Boone asked.

"We did. It's difficult to get good prints from cloth, so we were unsuccessful. Our lab guys are pretty sure that there are no prints. Looks like the thief wore gloves and was very careful. No prints on the tablets, none on the cap, none at the crime scene."

"Do you plan to charge Theo?" Mrs. Boone asked.

"We haven't made a decision yet," Hamilton said. "But it's safe to say we're headed that way."

The Boones absorbed this, and said nothing. Mr. Boone exhaled and looked at the ceiling. Mrs. Boone scribbled something on a legal pad. Theo was still fighting back tears. He knew he was innocent and telling the truth, but the police did not believe him. He wondered if his parents did.

Vorman broke the silence with still more bad news. "We'd like to search your house," he said.

Mr. and Mrs. Boone reacted in disbelief. "For what?" Mr. Boone demanded.

"For evidence," Vorman replied. "For the rest of the stolen goods."

"You can't treat us like common criminals," Mrs. Boone said angrily. "This is outrageous."

"We will not consent to a search," Mr. Boone said.

"We don't need your consent," Vorman said with a nasty smile. "We have a search warrant." He grabbed some folded papers from his coat pocket and slid them across the table. Mrs. Boone adjusted her reading glasses and read the two-page document. When she finished, she handed it to her husband. Theo wiped a tear with the back of his hand.

Chapter 14

For the next half hour, they haggled over the details. The air was thick with tension, and the exchanges between the detectives and Theo's parents were testy. It was finally agreed that the Boones would not enter their home until 5:00 p.m. that afternoon, at which time they would meet the detectives and other officers who would conduct the search.

The only words Theo could muster were, "It's a waste of time. There's nothing there." Both parents told him to be quiet.

After Hamilton and Vorman left, and Theo could finally speak, he reassured his parents that he was not involved in the crime in any way, and that a search was a waste of time. All three were stunned by the turn of events. Theo had never seen his parents so confused, and even frightened. They agreed they would seek the advice of a criminal defense lawyer, a friend, and Mrs. Boone left the conference room to make a call.

At 2:00 p.m., Mr. Boone drove Theo back to the school where they met with Mrs. Gladwell. Theo apologized for fighting. Mr. Boone said he and Mrs. Boone understood the decision to suspend Theo, and had no problems with it. They were disappointed, of course, but supported Mrs. Gladwell. Afterward, Theo got his bike, found his tires unslashed, and rode back to the office.

His parents were busy with clients and urgent legal matters. They closed their doors and seemed to forget about Theo. Elsa, Vince, and Dorothy were also preoccupied with piles of paperwork that were far more fascinating than chatting with a thirteen-year-old. Or, perhaps Theo was being too sensitive. He and Judge finally retreated to his office where he attempted to plow through some homework. Nothing happened. He couldn't take his mind off Spike Hock, a kid who lived one block away who was caught selling drugs in the ninth grade and spent eighteen very unpleasant months in a juvenile detention center two hundred miles away. Though Theo did not know Spike and had never spoken to him, he had heard many stories of his life behind chain-link fencing and razor wire. Gangs, beatings, cruel guards, a long ugly list. Spike never got his act together and fell back into the street life. Theo had been in court when Spike, at the age of seventeen, was sentenced as an adult to twenty years in prison for a multitude of crimes. Spike testified, begged for mercy, and blamed his troubles on the bad conditions he endured in the juvenile detention center.

Spike was a tough kid from the streets. Theo was not. Theo was a nice kid from a good family, a Boy Scout, an A student with plenty of friends. How was he supposed to survive locked away with gang members and tough guys? Separated from his parents, his friends, Judge. He was overwhelmed with fear and could think of nothing else. He stretched out on Judge's little bed, and, fortunately, fell asleep beside his dog.

A beeping cell phone awakened him. It was April Finnemore. "Theo, where are you?" she asked nervously.

"At the office," he said, jumping to his feet. "What's up?"

"I'm in Animal Court with my mom and Miss Petunia. We need your help."

"I think I'm sort of confined right now."

"Come on, Theo. We're really scared and need you. It won't take long."

"I didn't say I would help this woman."

"I know, Theo, I know. But she's really upset and needs a friend. Please, Theo. She can't afford a real lawyer and, well, she's been crying for the past hour. Please."

Theo thought for a second. No one had specifically ordered him to remain at the office. Everyone else was super busy and probably wouldn't miss him. "Okay," he said, and slapped his phone shut.

"Stay here, Judge," he said, then eased out of the back door, ran around to the front of the building, and quietly got his bike off the front porch. Ten minutes later he was parking it at the bike rack in front of the courthouse.

Miss Petunia grew flowers and herbs in a yard behind her small cottage just outside the city limits of Strattenburg. Every Saturday morning from March through October, she hauled her plants to the city Farmer's Market in Levi Park near the river. There, she joined dozens of farmers, gardeners, florists, fishermen, dairymen, producers, and other vendors who displayed their goods in booths that were arranged in neat rows on small patches of land that were carefully divided and regulated. Because Miss Petunia had been selling her flowers and herbs for many years, she had perhaps the best booth, one next to the entrance to the market. Next door to her was the booth run by May Finnemore, April's eccentric mother, who made and sold goat cheese. Miss Petunia was pretty weird, too, and naturally the women had become close friends over the years.

The market was wildly popular in Strattenburg, and on a bright Saturday morning half of the town would be there. Virtually anything edible could be found. Crispino's Tortilla Hut was the all-time favorite, with a long line forming by 10:00 a.m. Martha Lou sold her "World Famous" ginger cookies by the pound and always attracted a mob. Many of the vendors relied on the market to show a profit for the year, and there was a waiting list of those wanting booths.

Because Mrs. Boone spent little time in the kitchen, the family was not attracted to the market. Theo and his father played eighteen holes of golf on Saturday mornings, teeing off at 9:00 and having lunch at 1:00. To Theo, this was far more important than buying tomatoes and veggie burgers.

Miss Petunia was having trouble with the law because of her beloved pet llama, Lucy. April had mentioned the matter to Theo the day before during lunch, but he had been too preoccupied with his own troubles to worry about Miss Petunia's. At April's request, though, he had done some research into the city's laws and ordinances. He had passed this along to April and considered the matter closed, as far as he was concerned.

Certain that he was already a marked man and the subject of gossip all over town, and especially around the courthouse, Theo entered through a side door and hustled down a back stairway. Animal Court was in the basement, a fitting place for the lowest court in town. Real lawyers tried to avoid it. People with complaints could act as their own lawyers, and that is what attracted Theo to it. On most days anyway. Today, though, Theo was not excited about making an appearance in court.

For the first time in his life, the word "court" meant a place to be avoided.

He entered the door for Animal Court and walked inside. There was a dusty aisle down the middle of the room with folding chairs on both sides. To his right, Theo saw April, her mother, May, and a third person he assumed to be Miss Petunia. She had purple hair and round granny glasses with bright-orange frames. April had described her as "weirder than my mother."

Theo sat down and began whispering with the women.

Judge Yeck was not on the bench. Across the aisle, several people were waiting. One was Buck Boland, or Buck Baloney as he was better known, and he was wearing his standard tight-fitting dark brown uniform, one issued by All-Pro Security. Buck wore the uniform everywhere, on duty or off, and he'd been wearing it last Monday morning when he stopped Theo as he cut across his backyard. He had grabbed Theo's bike and threatened him. Earlier, he had thrown a rock at Theo, and now Buck glared across the aisle as if he would like to strangle him.

Judge Yeck's ancient clerk sat at a table in one corner, doing her crossword and trying to stay awake. After a few minutes, Judge Yeck walked through the door behind his bench and said, "Remain seated." No one had attempted to stand. Formalities were dispensed with in Animal Court, also known as Kitty Court. The judge was wearing his usual outfit—jeans, combat boots, no tie, an old sports coat, and he conducted himself with his usual disdain for his job. He had once been in a law firm but couldn't keep a job. He ran Animal Court because no one else would do it.

"Well, well," he began with a smile, "it's Mr. Boone again."

Theo stood and said, "Hello, Judge. Always nice to see you."

"And you. Who's your client?"

"Miss Petunia Plankmore, the owner of the animal."

Judge Yeck looked at some papers, then looked at Buck Baloney. "And who's Mr. Boland?"

"That's me," Buck said.

"Very well. The parties can come forward and we'll try and work things out." Theo knew the routine, and he and Miss Petunia stepped through the small gate in the bar and took a seat at a table closer to the judge. Buck followed them and sat as far away as possible. When they were in place, Judge Yeck said, "Mr. Boland, you have filed this complaint against Miss Petunia. You go first. Keep your seat and tell us what happened."

Buck looked around nervously, then plunged in. "Well, Judge, I work for All-Pro Security and we have the contract for the Farmer's Market."

"Why are you wearing a gun?" the judge asked.

"I'm a security guard."

"I don't care."

"And I have a permit."

"I don't care. I don't allow guns in my courtroom. Please remove it."

Buck grabbed his holster and snapped it off his belt. He placed it and the gun on the table.

"Up here," Judge Yeck said, pointing to a spot on his bench. Buck awkwardly stepped forward and placed the gun right where he was told. It was a very large pistol.

"Now go on," Yeck said when Buck returned to his seat.

"And so anyway, it's my job to provide security at the Farmer's Market. There are two of us, me and Frankie. He works the west end, and I watch the front. Been doing it for a few months. And Miss Petunia here has a booth near the front entrance where she sells flowers and herbs, and right next to her booth is a small open area where she keeps her llama."

"That would be Lucy?" Judge Yeck asked.

"Yes, sir. Two Saturdays ago I was walking by her booth, same as always, just doing my job, you know, when this llama walks up and stares at me. We're about on the same eye level, me and the llama, and at first I thought she might try and kiss me."

"The llama kisses people?" Judge Yeck interrupted.

"She's a very sweet llama, loves people, or most people," Miss Petunia blurted.

Judge Yeck looked at her and politely, but firmly, said, "You'll get your chance in a moment. Please do not interrupt."

"Sorry, Judge."

"Continue."

Buck sucked in his ample gut and went on: "Yes, sir, the llama kisses people, especially little kids. Kinda gross if you ask me, but there's usually some folks hanging around to get a better look at the llama, and occasionally she'll sort of lean down and kiss one of them."

"Okay, okay. We've established that Lucy the llama likes to kiss people. Now move on."

"Yes, sir. Well, like I said, the llama walked up to me. We stared at each other for a few seconds, then the llama raised her nose straight up, which means she's not happy, then she sort of cocked back her head and spit in my face. A lot of spit, too, not just a couple of drops. It was gross, sticky and smelly."

"The llama spits at people?" Judge Yeck asked, amused.

"Oh, yes, Judge, and she did it real quick like. I had no idea what was coming."

April's mother, May Finnemore, was a loud woman with rough manners who could be counted on to do the wrong thing. She laughed, and made no effort to conceal it.

"That's enough," Judge Yeck said sternly, though he himself seemed ready to chuckle. "Please continue, Mr. Boland."

"Got it."

"There were some kids watching, and I think they knew this llama was a spitter, and as soon as she spit in my face the kids cracked up laughing. It was very embarrassing and it made me mad, so, after I wiped my face off, I walked over to Miss Petunia and told her what happened. She said, 'Well, Lucy doesn't like you.' And I said, 'I don't care if she likes me or not, she can't be spitting at people, especially security personnel.' She didn't apologize or anything, in fact, I think she thought it was funny."

"Is this llama on a leash or confined in some way?" Judge Yeck asked.

"No, sir, it is not. It just sort of hangs around Miss Petunia's booth. There are always some kids petting it and making a fuss. So we discussed the matter for a few minutes and I realized the owner was not going to do anything about it, so I decided to walk away, to cool off and to wash my face. But I kept an eye on the llama, and I think she kept an eye on me. Part of my job is to watch the front entrance. Sometimes people will try and leave with stuff they haven't paid for, so I gotta keep 'em honest, you know what I mean, Judge?"

"Of course."

"And so anyway, about a half an hour later, I'm doing my job and I walk past her booth again. Didn't say a word to her or to the llama. I stopped and I was talking to Mr. Dudley Bishop and I felt something behind me. He stopped talking. I turned around and there was the llama again, staring at me. Before I could back away, she spit in my face for the second time. It was just as gross as the first time. Dudley is here as my witness."

From a folding chair in the audience, Mr. Dudley Bishop raised his hand.

"Is all this true, Mr. Bishop?" the judge asked.

"Every word of it," the witness replied.

"Continue."

"Well, I was pretty upset. People were laughing at me and everything, so I wiped my face off and went over to Miss Petunia. She had seen it happen and she was not at all concerned. She told me to stay away from the llama and things would be fine. I explained that I had a right to do my job and the problem was hers, not mine. Do something with her lousy llama. But she refused. I cooled off again and tried to keep my distance. If I got close to the entrance, the llama would stop whatever it was doing and give me a dirty look. I talked to Frankie about it and suggested we swap places for the rest of the morning, but he wanted no part of the llama. He said I should call Animal Control, which I did. The officer came out and had a chat with Miss Petunia. She said there is no city ordinance requiring llamas to be on a leash or confined in some way, and the Animal Control officer agreed with her. I guess it's okay for llamas to roam the city at will, spitting at people."

"I didn't realize this was a problem in Strattenburg," Judge Yeck observed.

"Well it is now. And there's more to the story, Judge."

"Continue."

"Well, last Saturday it happened again, only worse. I was keeping my distance from the animal, doing my job as best I could, trying to avoid it and not even making eye contact. I didn't say a word to Miss Petunia or anybody else around there. The other lady there, Mrs. Finnemore, has the booth next to the flower stall where she sells goat cheese, and she has this spider monkey who hangs around, attracting customers and increasing sales, I think."

"What does the monkey have to do with the llama?"

"I'll tell you. Sometimes the monkey will sit on the llama's back, sort of ride it around, and this always gets a lot of attention. Kids hang around and take pictures. Some of the parents even take photos of their kids posing with the llama and the monkey. Well, this one little girl got scared and started screaming. I walked over, and as soon as the llama saw me she bolted and ran at me. I didn't get within thirty feet of her, but she attacked anyway. I didn't want to get spit on again, so I moved back. She kept coming, with the monkey hanging on like some cowboy. When I realized the llama meant business, I turned around and started running. The faster I ran, the faster the llama ran. I could hear the monkey squealing, having fun, I guess. This was about eight o'clock, so the market was packed and everyone was laughing. I didn't know if the thing would bite or whatever. I thought about grabbing my gun and defending myself, but there were too many people around, plus I didn't want to kill the llama. We ran up and down the aisles, all over the market, people were laughing, the monkey was squealing, it was awful."

Judge Yeck raised a file to partially cover his face and hide the fact that he was about to burst out laughing. Theo glanced around the room and everyone was amused.

"It's not funny, Judge," Buck said.

"Continue."

"Well, it all came to an end when I fell down. I stumbled in front of Butch Tucker's watermelon stand, and before I could get up the llama bent down and spit at me. It missed my face but got my shirt wet. Butch is here if you want to verify this."

Butch raised his hand. "It's all true, Judge. I was there," he said with a grinning face.

"Thank you. Continue, please."

Buck was breathing hard and his face had turned red. He said, "Well, I finally got to my feet and I was ready to slug the llama, and maybe the monkey, too, when Frankie came running up with a stick and shooed the llama away. I guess it went back to its spot. I don't know. I was too upset. You gotta do something, Judge. I have the right to do my job without being attacked."

"Anything more?"

"I guess not. That's all for now."

"Any cross-examination, Mr. Boone?"

Theo decided it would be best for his client to tell her side of the story. He knew from experience that Judge Yeck did not like the usual courtroom procedures. "Let's hear from Miss Petunia," he said.

"A good idea. Miss Petunia, please give us your version."

Miss Petunia jumped to her feet, ready to defend Lucy.

"You can keep your seat," the judge said.

"I prefer to stand," she said.

"Then please stand."

"Thank you, Judge. All of what he said is true, but he left out a few things. Llamas spit when they feel threatened or harassed, and they do so as a means of defense, to protect themselves. They don't bite and they don't kick. They are very peaceful animals who've been around for thousands of years. They're from the same family as the camel, did you know that, Judge?"

"I did not."

"Well, they are, and they're hard working, loyal, and easy to care for. I've had Lucy for twelve years, and she pulls my wagon to the market every Saturday morning at sunrise. My car is tiny, and I can't use it to haul my flowers and herbs, so Lucy does it for me."

Judge Yeck held up a hand, looked at Theo, and asked, "Is it legal for a llama to pull a wagon on city streets?"

Theo replied, "Yes, sir. There is no ordinance against it."

"Where does this llama live?"

"In my backyard," Miss Petunia said. "I have a big backyard."

"Does the city allow llamas to be kept at private homes?"

Theo replied, "No, Your Honor. However, Miss Petunia does not live in the city. Her home is just outside the city limits, in the county, and the county does not prohibit a llama from living in her backyard."

"Thank you, Counselor. Please continue, Miss Petunia."

"A few months ago, Lucy and I were going home after the market was over, and we were stopped by a patrol car. Two policemen got out and started asking questions. They accused us of blocking traffic and other nonsense, but I think they were just curious. It really upset Lucy. She felt threatened."

"Did she spit on them?" Judge Yeck asked.

"No, sir."

"How often does she spit on people?"

"It rarely happens, Judge. About a year ago, the guy who reads the electric meters came around the house and wouldn't leave her alone. She got him. He was wearing a uniform of sorts. You see, Judge, I don't think Lucy likes large men in uniforms. She feels threatened by them. She's never spat on a woman or a child, or a man who was not in a uniform."

"A gold star for her."

"And Mr. Boland here has not been that kind to her. He's stopped by several times, throwing his weight around, trying to tell me that Lucy needed to be on a leash, or kept in a certain place, stuff like that. He thinks he's in charge of the entire market. He gets part of the blame for this."

"That's not true, Your Honor," Buck said. However, anyone who watched Buck in uniform knew immediately that he was proud of his authority.

"We're not going to bicker. Are you finished, Miss Petunia?"

"I guess."

"All right. Mr. Boland, what, exactly, do you want me to do?"

"Well, Judge, I think she should keep her llama at home, in the backyard, where it can't spit on people or attack them in public."

Theo said, "But, Judge, she has to get her flowers and herbs to market, and there's no law against using her llama to pull her wagon. It would be unfair to require my client to keep Lucy at home."

"Maybe, but something must be done, Mr. Boone," Judge Yeck said. "We can't allow an animal like this to spit on people. Mr. Boland has the right to do his job without the fear of being assaulted by a llama. Do you agree, Mr. Boone?"

"Yes, I do, and on behalf of my client, I offer an apology to Mr. Boland for Lucy's actions." Apologies meant a lot to Judge Yeck, and Theo had insisted that they offer one. Miss Petunia was against the idea, but Theo prevailed.

Buck nodded his acceptance but was not satisfied.

"You got a plan, Mr. Boone?" Judge Yeck asked.

Theo stood and addressed the judge. "Let's try this. Next Saturday morning, Mr. Boland here swaps places with the other guard, Frankie, and Frankie is instructed to stay as far away from Lucy as possible, and still do his job. If Lucy goes after Frankie, then we will agree to take more drastic measures."

"Such as?"

"Your Honor, Lucy has never been on a leash, but my client will give it a try. Miss Petunia feels confident that she can talk to Lucy about this and convince her not to be so aggressive with large men in uniforms."

"How big is Frankie?" Judge Yeck asked Buck.

"A shrimp."

"Miss Petunia talks to Lucy?" Judge Yeck asked Theo.

Miss Petunia stood too and said, "Oh, yes, Judge. We chat all the time. Lucy is very intelligent. I think I can convince her to stop the spitting."

"Mr. Boland, what do you think of this idea?"

Buck realized he was not getting what he wanted, not on this day anyway, so he shrugged and said, "I'll give it a try. I'm not looking for trouble, Judge. But it's pretty embarrassing."

"I'm sure it is. We'll proceed with the plan, and if it doesn't work, we'll be back here next week. Agreed?"

Everyone agreed and nodded along.

"Animal Court is adjourned," Judge Yeck said.

Chapter 15

As soon as Theo left the courthouse, reality returned. For a short while, he had been able to forget his problems and lose himself in the wacky world of a spitting llama. Miss Petunia was thrilled. May Finnemore gave him an awkward hug. Most importantly, April was impressed by his courtroom skills.

But the fun was suddenly over, and Theo faced nothing but humiliation. He was being falsely accused, and stalked, and harassed, and now his entire family was being dragged into it. The very thought of a bunch of police officers picking through every room of the Boone home was terrifying. What would the neighbors think?

Then Theo had a thought that was so awful he had to

stop his bike and catch his breath. He sat down on an empty bus bench and stared at the asphalt pavement. If someone were mean enough and reckless enough to stash stolen goods in his locker, why wouldn't they do the same thing at his house? The garage doors were usually left open. There was a storage shed in the rear, and they never locked its door. It would not be too difficult for some creep to sneak around the exterior of their home and find an unnoticed spot to hide a few more tablets, or cell phones, or even laptops.

What if the police found such items? Caught again, red-handed! At some point, Theo wondered if his own parents might become suspicious of him.

He eventually got on his bike and continued to the office, where he eased through the rear door and found Judge asleep under his desk. He tiptoed down the hall and managed to avoid seeing anyone. Elsa was tidying up her desk and preparing to leave. She was subdued and worried about Theo, and he felt worse after chatting with her.

The clock inched closer to 5:00 p.m.

The police were waiting, at the curb in front of 886 Mallard Lane, home of Woods and Marcella Boone and their only child, Theo, who had never lived anywhere else. They were waiting in two unmarked cars, and for this the Boones were thankful. Two police cruisers adorned with all the bells and whistles would have attracted neighbors like a magnet.

Theo wheeled in first on his bike, with his parents right behind him. Detectives Vorman and Hamilton approached from the street and introduced officers Mabe and Jesco, both in plainclothes. They were invited inside where Mrs. Boone made a pot of coffee and everybody else sat around the kitchen table. While the coffee was brewing, Mr. Boone slowly read the search warrant again, then handed it to Mrs. Boone who did the same.

"I fail to see why it's necessary to search every room in the house," Mr. Boone said.

"It's not necessary," Mrs. Boone added sharply. Their anger was clear, but under control, for the moment anyway.

Hamilton said, "I agree. We don't plan to be here all night. We would like to take a look at Theo's room and maybe a couple others, then the garage, the basement, maybe the attic."

"There's nothing in my room," Theo said. He was standing in the doorway, watching and listening.

"That's enough, Theo," his father said.

"You plan to go through our attic?" Mrs. Boone asked in disbelief as she poured coffee.

"Yes," Hamilton replied.

"Good luck. You may not make it out alive."

"Do you have any outbuildings?" Vorman asked.

"There's a storage shed out back," Mr. Boone said.

"What's in it?"

"I don't keep a list. The usual stuff. A lawn mower, garden hoses, Weed Eater, old furniture."

"Do you keep it locked?"

"Never."

Theo blurted again, "There's nothing in the attic and nothing in the storage shed. You're wasting your time because you have the wrong suspect."

The six adults stared at him, then his father said, "Okay, Theo. That's enough."

"Well, I agree with Theo," his mother said. "This is a waste of time and effort. The longer you suspect Theo the longer it will take to find the real criminal."

"We're just doing our investigation," Hamilton said. "It's our job."

Theo's room was in surprisingly good shape. His parents gave demerits for an unmade bed, or clothes on the floor, or books off the shelves. Demerits translated into a reduction in his weekly allowance, so, to Theo, some serious cash was on the line if he didn't tidy things up. It was agreed that Mrs. Boone would stay with the officers in the room and monitor the search. A ten-minute inspection revealed nothing, and the search party moved to the guest bedroom and its closets, then to the den. With Mrs. Boone watching every move, the officers carefully looked into cabinets and shelves. They gently touched every item in a coat closet. They almost tiptoed through the house, as if they were afraid they might break something.

After they left the den, Theo and his father turned on the television and watched the local news. Theo tried to appear relaxed, but he could think of nothing but the storage shed and how easy it would be to hide the loot out there. His stomach ached and he wanted to lie down, but he tried gamely to look nonchalant. What if he heard them yell, "We found it!" or "Here it is!"? His life would be over.

Mrs. Boone led them to the basement where they searched the laundry room, a game room, and a utility room. Nothing. She led them to the attic, cramped and stuffed with boxes of the typical useless junk that would eventually be thrown away.

"Does Theo come up here often?" Hamilton asked Mrs. Boone.

"Only when he hides stolen goods," she replied. Hamilton vowed to ask no more questions.

It took almost an hour to open all the cardboard

boxes and storage bins. Finding nothing, they moved to the garage and searched another utility room and a large closet housing the heating and air-conditioning units. While they were out of the house, Theo asked his father, "Can I go to my room, Dad?"

"Sure."

As Theo was leaving the den, his father said, "Theo, your mother and I believe you one hundred percent. Do you understand this?"

"I do. Thanks, Dad."

Upstairs, Theo stretched out on his bed and patted a spot next to him. Judge was waiting for the signal and hopped up on the bed—a no-no in the eyes of Mrs. Boone. But the door was locked and Theo was safe from the world, for the moment anyway. He heard a noise from the backyard and knew the search party was poking around the storage shed. He waited, tried to relax, and tried to shake the feeling that his room had just been invaded by the police.

Minutes passed and there were no excited noises from outside. Nothing unusual was found in the storage shed, and after two hours the search ended. The police thanked Mr. and Mrs. Boone for their cooperation—as if they had a choice—and left Mallard Lane.

Mrs. Boone knocked on Theo's door and he opened it.

"They're gone," she said as she hugged him. "Are you okay?"

"No, not really."

"Neither am I. Look, Theo, I'm a pretty good lawyer. So is your father. We're determined to protect you and make sure nothing bad happens, okay? The detectives are good men who are just doing their jobs. They will eventually find the truth, and this nightmare will be over. I promise you there will be a happy ending."

"If you say so, Mom."

"Your father has a great idea. Since you don't have school tomorrow, let's go to Santo's and get a pizza."

Theo managed to smile.

As they were driving away, Theo, from the backseat, asked, "Say, have you guys ever heard of a spitting llama?"

"No," his parents replied in unison.

"Have I got a story for you."

Chapter 16

Late Friday morning, when he should have been in third-period Government, Theo finally got bored with his suspension and admitted to himself that he missed school. His mother was in court. His father was buried in paperwork at his desk. No one in the law firm had time for him, so he informed Elsa that he was going to visit Ike. She gave him a hug and once again looked as though she might cry. Theo was so sick of all this pity.

Judge ran along behind him as he pedaled through Strattenburg, being careful to avoid the busy streets because the last thing he wanted was to get stopped by a cop or a truant officer. Kids were caught all the time skipping school, and serious truants were hauled into Youth Court. Theo had a hunch that he was about to see more of Youth Court than he had ever dreamed. And the way his luck was running this week, he was almost certain another cop would stop him.

He made it safely to Ike's office, though, and bounded up the steps to a wonderfully messy room where his cranky old uncle barely earned enough money to survive. In spite of his cluttered desk and his Boone-like fondness of work, Ike did not really push himself. He lived alone in a small apartment. He drove an old Spitfire with a million miles on it. He didn't need much, so he didn't work much. Especially on Fridays. Theo knew from experience that most lawyers ran out of gas around noon on Friday. The courthouse was much quieter. It was hard to find a judge on Friday afternoon. The clerks took longer lunch breaks and began sneaking away as soon as possible.

Ike, though no longer a real lawyer, certainly followed this tradition. He slept late, something he did almost every day, and puttered around his office until the crack of noon when he walked downstairs to the Greek deli for lunch. To start the weekend properly, Ike had two glasses of wine with his Friday lunch.

Theo and Judge arrived around 10:30, and Ike, after three cups of coffee, was hyper and talkative. "I have a suspect, Theo, not a real person, not a name, not yet, but I have an idea that we must pursue. Are you with me?"

"Sure, Ike."

"First, though, I want to hear all about the fight. Every detail. Every kick, punch, bloody nose. Tell me you punched some little thug in the face."

Ike's feet were on his desk—dirty sandals, no socks. So Theo kicked back in his chair and put his feet on the desk, too. "Well, it happened real fast," he began, and launched into a long and fairly accurate account of the fight. Ike was grinning, a very proud uncle. Theo did not embellish much, and he resisted the temptation to improve his skills as a brawler. When he finished describing the meeting with Mrs. Gladwell, and the suspension, Ike said, "Good for you, Theo. Sometimes you have no choice. Wear the suspension like a badge of honor."

"Did you hear about the search warrant?" Theo asked, anxious to share all of the week's adventures.

"What search warrant?" Ike demanded. Theo told that story, and Ike never stopped shaking his head. To lighten things up, Theo asked, "Have you ever heard of a spitting llama?" Ike had not, so Theo recounted in great detail his latest adventure in Animal Court.

When the story time was over, Ike jumped to his feet, cracked his knuckles, and said, "Okay, Theo. Our task is to find the person who's trying to frame you, right?"

"Right."

"I've thought about nothing else for the past forty-eight hours. Tell me what you know so far."

"Not much. My dad is convinced that it's someone from inside the school, most likely another student because an adult would have a hard time getting into my locker without being suspicious. He thinks it's more than one kid."

"I agree completely. Who's your number one suspect?"

"I don't have one, Ike. My parents have pushed me to make a list of all the kids who may have a grudge. I'm not saying I'm the greatest guy at school, but I really can't think of anyone who would, (a) break into my locker and steal stuff on Monday, then, (b) break in and rob the computer store Tuesday night, leaving the cap behind, then, (c) break into my locker again on Wednesday and plant the stolen tablets, all in an effort to get me thrown in jail. Somebody out there really, really hates me, and I just can't think of who it might be."

"That's because you don't know him. You've probably never met him. Maybe you've seen him, but you don't know it."

Ike was pacing back and forth behind his desk, scratching his gray beard, frowning in deep thought.

"Okay," Theo replied. "Who is it?"

Ike suddenly sat down and leaned across his desk, staring at Theo with glowing eyes. "Your parents are lawyers, and good ones. Lawyers take cases that involve people who are mad, upset, hurt, in trouble, ticked off enough to spend a lot of money filing a lawsuit. Now, your father is a real estate lawyer, which is a pretty dull way to make a living if you ask me. He does a lot of paperwork. He deals with people who are buying and selling homes, buildings, land, you know what I'm talking about."

"I'm not going to be a real estate lawyer," Theo said.

"Attaboy. My point being he does not deal with clients who are engaged in conflict. Right?"

"Right."

"Your mother, on the other hand, deals with nothing but conflict, and the worst kind. Divorces. Marriages blow up. Husbands and wives fighting over who gets custody of the kids, who gets the house, the cars, the furniture, the money. Charges of adultery, abuse, neglect. Terrible cases sometimes, Theo. I never had the stomach for divorce. Your mother, though, is one of the best. Always has been."

Theo was nodding, listening, waiting. He knew all of this.

Ike tapped his fingertips together and said, "A divorce is an awful thing for a child, Theo. The two people he loves most suddenly can't live together, they no longer love each other, in fact they often hate each other, and in the process of splitting up they use the child as a prize to fight over.

For the child, it is traumatic, bewildering, and quite painful. The child is not sure which parent will get custody, so the child does not know where he/she will be living. Often, the husband and wife are forced to sell the family home. Sometimes the child prefers one parent over another and is forced to choose. Imagine, Theo, being forced to choose whether you want to live with your mother or your father. A divorce is an emotional shock for a child, and the damage lasts for a long time." He paused to scratch his beard. Then, "I think your problems are linked to one of your mother's divorce cases. I think one of her clients has a kid in your school, and this kid secretly hates you because he doesn't like the way the divorce is going. Since your mother always represents the wife, and the wife almost always gets custody of the children, maybe this kid doesn't like his mother and wants to live with his father, who, for obvious reasons, really doesn't like Marcella Boone. This intense dislike of your mother is not at all unusual in divorce cases, and it's probably shared with the children who are caught in the crossfire."

Two bricks, one on each shoulder, suddenly vanished into the air, and Theo felt much lighter. What a brilliant idea! And one that had never occurred to Theo. But Ike, the wise old uncle, could see it all.

He continued: "You may wonder why Marcella hasn't mentioned this. She has probably given it some thought, but your mother is such a zealous advocate for her clients that she often does not see the big picture. And, she is such a professional that she would never consider giving away the secrets of her clients."

"Not even to protect her own son?"

"Sure, Theo, if your mother thought you might be harmed by someone involved in one of her cases, I have no doubt she would do everything possible to protect you. But lawyers such as your mother can become so determined to protect their clients that they develop blind spots. They don't see what others might see. And, you have to admit, Theo, this is some pretty outrageous behavior by our mystery kid. Not exactly the type of behavior that could be anticipated by your mother or anyone else for that matter. Your mother has handled so many divorces for so many years she probably doesn't think about grudges being carried by the children of her clients."

"Do I have a chat with my mother?"

"And ask her what? Who's in the middle of a bad divorce, with kids at your school? Suppose she can think of a couple of cases. Suppose you narrow the list of suspects. Somehow, not sure exactly, but let's say you're able to prove the mystery kid is the real culprit. The kid gets arrested for burglarizing the computer store, kicked out of school, all the bad stuff that he deserves. You're off the hook and the kid's in big trouble, right?"

"Right."

"There is the possibility your mother could get into some trouble herself. Her client will not be happy with her because she's responsible, in part, for the client's kid getting into a serious jam. I mean, this kid will do time in a detention facility, and the finger might be pointed at your mother. Sure the kid's guilty and should be punished, but the client will feel as though your mother violated her privacy. It puts your mother in a dicey situation."

"You have a plan?"

"Always. Did you bring your laptop?"

Theo patted his backpack and said, "Right here."

"Good. Let's go online and check the cases filed in Family Court. Make a list of all of the current divorce cases in which your mother is the lawyer. We'll go through the most active ones and make a list of those in which there are kids involved, kids who go to your school. At that point, the list should be pretty short."

Theo was already unloading his laptop. "This is a brilliant idea, Ike."

"We'll see."

The Family Court clerk's docket divided divorces into various categories: Contested-Uncontested; Active-Inactive; Children-No Children; In Discovery-Awaiting Trial. After half an hour, with Theo on his laptop and Ike pecking away at his bulky desktop, they had a list of twenty-one active divorce cases in which Marcella Boone represented the wife. Of those, three were in the No Children category and therefore removed from the list. Five more were in the Uncontested category, and Ike felt as though these could be eliminated, too. Uncontested divorces were much easier and quicker and did not create the raw feelings that would lead someone to slash tires and throw rocks through windows.

"What does 'Secured' mean?" Theo asked as they scanned the records.

"It means trouble for us," Ike said. "I had forgotten about the Secured Docket. There are some divorce cases in which the claims of bad conduct are particularly nasty, and either party can ask the judge to secure the file, which means it's locked away and is only available to the attorneys involved. Nothing is made public. It could be our dead end, unless, of course, we have access to your mother's files. But let's keep going."

Ike made a list of the client's last names involved in

the thirteen cases on their list, and Theo downloaded the directory of students at Strattenburg Middle School. Cross-checking, the list shrunk to about half, with a possible seven cases involving kids in Theo's school. Some names were so common, though, that they could not be included or excluded. There was a Smith, a Johnson, a Miller, and a Green. Looking at the names, Theo felt somewhat relieved. He did not know any of the kids with the last names on the list.

Two years earlier, when Theo was in the sixth grade, a girl named Nancy Griffin told him his mother had been her mother's lawyer in a recent divorce. The divorce was over, final, and Mrs. Griffin was quite pleased with the work Theo's mother had done. This was the first time Theo realized Mrs. Boone's job could affect his friends and classmates. He later asked his mother about it and demanded to know why she had not informed him. Mrs. Boone carefully, and sternly, explained that lawyers work with certain ethical rules, and one of the most important is complete secrecy about a client's business.

Ike scribbled on a legal pad, and said, "So we have a possibility of seven names, or seven divorce cases being handled by your mother with the kids in your school. Recognize anyone?"

"Not really. There's a kid named Tony Green in the

seventh grade, but we don't know if he's in the right Green family. Other than that, nothing looks familiar."

"Let's go back to the Secured Docket," Ike said, and Theo was there a good ten seconds before his uncle. There were eight cases under lock and key, and identified only by the last name of the wife or husband who had filed the lawsuit for divorce. The names of the attorneys were not listed.

Ike said, "You gotta figure that the divorce we're looking for is a nasty one. The parents are fighting for custody, and our mystery kid prefers to live with his father. Otherwise, he wouldn't be attacking the son of his mother's lawyer. Make sense?"

"I guess."

"For a father to gain custody, he must prove the mother is unfit to raise the kids. The law always prefers the mother, and it's rare that the father gets custody."

"I know," Theo said.

"To prove a mother unfit, the father has to come up with all sorts of bad behavior on the part of the mother. Those cases often end up being protected by the Secured Docket, and for obvious reasons."

"Then we're out of luck."

"Yes, unless we could take a peek at your mother's files."

"Are you crazy?"

"Yes, Theo, I'm crazy, been that way for some time now. And I'll do crazy things to find out who's stalking you, harassing you, and trying to get you convicted of a serious crime. Call me crazy, but maybe it's time to break some rules. You got in a fight yesterday and broke a rule. But, you really had no choice, right?"

"Right, I guess."

"I'm not talking about breaking the law, Theo. It would not be illegal to look at Marcella's files. Might be a bit unethical, but we're not going to give away sensitive information. And, it might be the only way to solve this little mystery."

"I don't know, Ike."

"What type of digital storage system does the firm use?"

"It's called InfoBrief, a pretty basic system, just for storage, cataloging, and cutting down on paper."

"Who has access to it?"

"Not me. My parents, Dorothy and Vince, and Elsa, but my dad and Dorothy rarely use it. My mom and Vince use it as a way to keep everything in order and find stuff without digging through a bunch of paperwork. Plus it has all the legal research built in."

"Can you get a password?"

Theo thought about this for a long time. If he got the password, and gave it to Ike, then he would be an accomplice to something. Not a crime, maybe, but certainly something he would rather avoid. He was in enough hot water already. The last thing he wanted was his mother yelling at him for violating her clients' privacy.

"Look, Ike, I'll just go to my mom and tell her what I think. I'll lay out our theory, and ask for her help. She is my mother, you know?"

"That's a great idea, Theo, and it makes good sense. But don't do it right now. Let's see if we can crack this case without getting her involved. I don't want to ask Marcella Boone to give me sensitive information about a client."

"Is this a long shot, Ike?"

"Maybe, but it's the best theory so far. The police are not looking at anyone else because they're convinced you're the thief. They might show up any day now with a warrant to haul you into Youth Court. If we don't find the real criminal soon, Theo, this situation will get much worse. Do you understand?"

"Yes, believe me, I understand."

"Listen to me, Theo. A long time ago, I was a successful lawyer in Strattenburg, had an office just down the hall from your mother, had lots of clients, and life was good. Then the cops showed up and started asking questions. I didn't have all the answers. They came back with more questions, then more. I couldn't believe what was happening and I slowly realized I was headed for trouble, but I couldn't stop it. Once the criminal justice system starts moving against you, it's hard to stop. Believe me, Theo, I've been there. It's a rotten feeling. The sky is falling and there's no place to hide."

It was the first time Ike had ever talked about his troubles, his past, and Theo was fascinated. He decided to ask the question he had always wanted to ask. "Were you guilty, Ike?"

Ike thought about this, and finally said, "I did some things wrong, Theo, things I'll always regret. You, on the other hand, have done nothing wrong, and that's why I don't mind breaking a few little rules to protect you. Let's get to the bottom of this, now, and get the police off your back."

"Okay, okay."

"Can you get me the password?"

"I think so."

Chapter 17

Again, Theo and Judge avoided the busy streets as they returned to the law offices of Boone & Boone. Theo was so deep in thought, and so thoroughly confused, that he ran a STOP sign and darted in front of a mail carrier. "Watch it, kid!" the man yelled, and Theo said, "Sorry," over his shoulder. Judge raced ahead, as if he wanted to keep his distance from Theo.

It was lunchtime, and Elsa and Dorothy were eating salads in the kitchen, both talking at the same time. Theo slipped by without being seen. His mother's office was empty. "Probably tied up in court," he mumbled to himself. Vince's door was open but he was gone. He usually left the building for lunch. His desktop was on, as always, with the screen saver visible.

The easiest way to "borrow" the password was to take it from one of the five PCs. Each lawyer had one, plus Vince, Dorothy, and Elsa. If Theo really believed he could go so far as "borrowing" a password, then this was the perfect opportunity. But, he was having a difficult time convincing himself that it was the right thing to do. Ike was convinced, but Theo wasn't Ike. Theo knew it was wrong, maybe not illegal, but certainly wrong.

The line between right and wrong had always been clear; now, though, nothing was clear. The wrongs were piling on top of him. It was wrong for someone to break into his locker and plant stolen loot with the obvious goal of getting him in serious trouble. It was wrong for someone to stalk him, to slash his tires and throw a rock through his window. Theo had done nothing wrong, yet he was now being treated like a criminal. The police had the wrong suspect. The police were wrong in not believing him, and if Theo were to be charged by the police, another wrong would occur. It was wrong for Theo to jump into the fight, though his father and Vince and Ike seemed to think it was not so wrong. Was it wrong for Theo to break an office rule and steal a password, all in an effort to prevent another, much larger wrong? Could doing something wrong lead to the right result?

It was all so confusing, but Theo trusted Ike, and Ike

had no doubt that taking the password was the right thing to do.

Theo led Judge back to his office and told him to take a nap. When the dog was situated, Theo eased down the hallway and listened for voices. Dorothy and Elsa were talking about recipes. No sound from his father upstairs—Woods Boone was known to take his own nap during lunch. Theo slipped into Vince's office, closed the door, and locked it. He sat in Vince's chair, and, careful not to disturb anything on his desk, examined his PC. The screen saver was a stock photo of a sunset over the ocean. Theo clicked on Main Menu, then on InfoBrief. A password was demanded, so he exited and went to My Computer. He clicked on Desktop, then Control Panel, then System and Security, then Passwords. Vince had a lot of passwords, and Theo felt like a creep for looking at them. Passwords for online retail accounts, cell phones, two dating sites, a travel site, fantasy football, and at least a dozen others. At the end of the list was InfoBrief, and Theo clicked on it. The password Avalanche88TeeBone33 appeared. Theo quickly wrote it down, then exited to Main Menu. He clicked on InfoBrief, entered the password, and the screen went blank for five seconds until "InfoBrief-Boone & Boone-Account Code: 647R" appeared. Theo wrote down the code and clicked on Enter. A long list of case names appeared, names such as *Denise Sneiter versus William B. Sneiter*, and Theo knew he had found his mother's divorce cases. He quickly exited, returned to the screen saver, and stood without touching anything else. He took a deep breath and turned the doorknob, certain that someone was outside just waiting to pounce on him. But the coast was clear, and he hurried back to his little office where his dog was still sleeping and everything was safe.

Theo knew that the InfoBrief account would record an entry at 12:14 p.m., Friday, from Vince's computer, but he doubted if it would be noticed anytime soon. If anyone questioned him, he would simply deny everything. It was, after all, Friday afternoon and there was a good chance neither Vince nor his mother nor anyone else would use InfoBrief until Monday morning, and, more importantly, the system's entry record was not something that was routinely pulled up and examined.

Though his little crime so far seemed perfect, Theo felt lousy about it. He debated whether he would actually give Ike the password and code, and as the minutes passed he was inclined not to. It was one thing to sneak around and lift them from Vince's lightly secured computer, but it was something far more serious for Ike to actually open the files and dig for sensitive information.

His mother arrived just before 1:00 p.m. She had brought lunch and they ate at the conference room table with Mr. Boone. The mood was somber and they talked about things other than Theo's mess. As he nibbled on a sandwich, he was tempted to bring up the idea that the conspiracy against him could be related to one of his mother's bad divorce cases, but Ike had told him to wait.

So he waited.

Theo was in his office, plowing through homework and watching the clock move slowly, when Elsa buzzed him through the phone intercom. "Theo, there's someone here to see you," she said.

"Who is it?" he asked, startled and then afraid the police were back.

"A friend."

Theo hurried to the front of the building. Standing awkwardly by Elsa's desk was Griff, who, when last seen the morning before, was receiving suspension from Mrs. Gladwell just like Theo. They walked into the conference room and Theo closed the door. They sat in the heavy leather chairs and Griff looked around the room. "Pretty cool," he said. "Is this yours?"

"I use it sometimes," Theo said. "I have a small office in the back."

After an awkward pause, Griff asked, "Did your parents yell at you?"

"Not too bad. What about you?"

"They weren't too happy. I'm grounded for a month, extra work around the house, no allowance for two weeks, but I guess it could've been worse."

"Sounds pretty bad."

"Look, Theo, the reason I'm here is that my parents want me to apologize for the fight. So, I apologize."

"No problem," Theo said. "I apologize, too. It was all pretty stupid, you know?"

"Yep, pretty stupid. Baxter's got a big mouth and it gets him in trouble."

"Baxter apologized, too. Let's forget about it."

"Done." Another pause, but Griff had something else on his mind. "Look, Theo, the rumor is that the cops think you broke into Big Mac's and stole a bunch of stuff and some of it was found in your locker. Is that right?"

Theo nodded.

"Well, I find it hard to believe because I don't think you would break into a store at night and steal stuff, you know. That's not like you."

"Tell that to the police."

"I will if you want me to."

"Thanks."

"Anyway, Big Mac has been telling people in the store that the police have caught the thief, Theodore Boone, and that they found three Linx 0-4 Tablets in your locker. I guess the guy's got a big mouth."

Theo's shoulders sunk and he looked out a window. "I guess he does."

"You wanna hear something strange? My sister Amy is in the tenth grade and she knows a guy named Benny. He's not a boyfriend or anything like that, just a friend. This guy Benny knows a guy named Gordy, and, according to Gordy, some guy offered to sell him an 0-4 Tablet for fifty dollars a couple of days ago at school, in the parking lot. Brand new, still in the box. Those things cost four hundred dollars, and this guy is trying to sell one for fifty. You gotta figure it's stolen, right?"

"Right," Theo said, suddenly staring at Griff. "What's his name?"

"I don't know, but I can probably find out. How many of the 0-4s were stolen?"

"I'm not sure, but I think more than three, along with some laptops and cell phones."

"Why would someone plant the stuff in your locker and then call the police?"

"That's the key question here, Griff, the one we're trying to answer. Look, there can't be too many stolen 0-4s on the black market out there. We need to get the name of the guy who's trying to sell them. And the sooner the better. Can you talk to your sister?"

"Sure I can."

"Please do it, Griff. And hurry."

Griff hustled away and Theo returned to his office. The suspension was really getting old.

At 3:45, his mother gave him permission to leave the office for personal reasons. Theo said good-bye to Judge and sped away on his bike. School was out, for the day and for the week, and other kids were loose on the streets of Strattenburg, ready to play and enjoy the short break. Theo was happy that the week was over. It had begun Monday with a slashed front tire and plunged straight downhill from there. He was also worried, and for obvious reasons. If he didn't find out who was after him, and quickly, the upcoming week could be even worse.

Major Ludwig was waiting in the basement of the VFW building, the home of Boy Scout Troop 1440. The meeting was scheduled to begin at 4:00 p.m. sharp, but the Major expected his scouts to arrive at least five minutes early. He despised tardiness and was known to bark and growl if you showed up late for anything. Theo arrived at 3:57. Brian and Edward, two friends from Mr. Mount's homeroom, were there, along with Sam, Isaac, and Bart, three seventh graders. All six Scouts had signed on for the Aviation merit badge, and Major Ludwig would be their counselor. He had flown fighter jets in the Marines and now worked part-time as a flight instructor at the city airport.

At first, Theo was a little awkward around Brian and Edward, his classmates. He wasn't sure if he should feel embarrassed, or proud. How much gossip was making the rounds at school in his absence? Plenty, he figured. The Major sensed the unease and wasted no time in discussing his plans.

"This is going to be very exciting," he began. "I've been flying for almost forty years, and I have loved every minute of it. We are going to study airplanes—piston engines, turboprops, and jets. We're going to build a model airplane, powered by batteries and able to climb to an altitude of two hundred feet. This will teach you the principles of flight—airspeed, lift, drag, aerodynamics—as well as the control surfaces—the ailerons, elevators, and rudder. You will learn how to read an aeronautical chart and plot a course for a real flight, a flight you will make using some really cool simulator software. We will visit the airport here in Strattenburg, look at various airplanes, then climb up into the tower and watch the air traffic controller as he directs traffic. There's not a lot of traffic here, but it will still be interesting to see how a controller handles things. Then, last but not least, when you've learned all the basics, we'll go for a real flight. With your parents' permission, I'll take you up two at a time in my little Cessna. We'll climb to about five thousand feet, and I'll let you handle the airplane. I'll keep my hands on the controls at all times, but you'll get a real good feel for the airplane. We'll do turns, climbs, and descents. We'll pick a beautiful day so you'll have a perfect bird's-eye view of where we live and the land around us. How about it, men? Sound like fun?"

The six boys were in a trance, thoroughly engrossed in their upcoming adventure. All six nodded eagerly. For the moment, Theo forgot about his problems. The Major handed out Aviation merit badge booklets and outlined the assignment for their meeting next Friday, then he picked up a large model airplane, the same one he used for real instruction, and began describing its various parts.

Theo, ever the dreamer, began thinking of how cool it would be to fly airplanes—fighter jets and 747s. What a great life—first the adventure of dogfights high above the battlefield, then traveling the world as the captain of a luxury commercial airliner. He had always wanted to be a lawyer, but right now the law had lost some of its appeal. Being a pilot seemed far more exciting.

At 5:00 p.m. sharp, the Major said the meeting was over.

When they gathered for the next meeting, he expected all assignments to be in perfect order. As the Scouts said their good-byes, he waited until they were almost out of the door when he said, "Say, Theo, could I have a word with you?"

"Sure, Major," Theo said. The other Scouts got on their bikes and left. Theo and the Major stood near the door.

"None of my business," the Major said, "but I hear things are not going too well, some kind of problem with the police involving a burglary. I'm not being nosy, Theo, I'm just concerned."

Theo nodded and for a second thought it would be wiser to reveal nothing. However, with his face plastered all over the Internet, his name linked to the crime, and his guilt already determined, it seemed silly acting as though he couldn't talk about it. "Yes, sir," he said. "It looks like I'm the number one suspect."

"So you've met with the police?"

"Several times." In fact, Theo could not remember how many times. "They don't believe me, and they seem determined to charge me with the crime."

"That's absurd, Theo."

"I sure think so."

"Look, Theo, I do some volunteer work in Youth Court. If a kid in trouble needs a volunteer, someone to listen to him and give him advice, the Court will appoint me to lend a hand. The kid has a lawyer, of course, but you know how busy lawyers are. I work with the lawyer to do what's best for the kid. My point is that I know both of the Youth Court judges very well. I'll be happy to get involved on your behalf if you would like, not as a volunteer because you don't need one, but as someone who can talk to the judges off the record. The idea of accusing you of a burglary is ridiculous."

Theo felt himself getting choked up, but managed to say, "Thanks, Major."

"I know you're innocent, Theo, and I'll do everything I can to help."

"Thanks," Theo said, trying to hide his emotions.

Chapter 18

The Major shook hands with Theo, gave him a pat on the back, and closed the door behind him. When Theo was outside he walked to his bike and got on it. He pushed off, felt something strange, and realized his front tire was flat.

A sharp pain hit low in his stomach, and Theo wasn't sure if it was anger or fear, or both. He looked around to see if anyone was watching, then he stared at the tire and thought about what he should do next. Nothing came to mind. He was so angry and confused his brain was a jumbled mess. Slowly, he got off his bike and looked at the front tire. The small gash looked familiar.

He decided not to bother the Major, so he began

pushing his bike through the parking lot of the VFW and onto the sidewalk. The more he walked, the clearer he could think. How many people knew he would be at a merit badge meeting on Friday afternoon at 4:00 p.m.? He suddenly had five suspects—the other Scouts. Brian and Edward from his homeroom, and Bart, Isaac, and Sam from the seventh grade. They had parked their bikes in the same rack Theo had parked his, and when his departure was delayed by the Major, there was the split-second opportunity for one of them to stick a knife in his front tire.

The law office was about ten blocks away, and Theo was tired. He called his father's cell phone, and, surprisingly, he answered. Woods Boone despised his cell phone and usually ignored it.

"Dad, it's me," Theo said.

"Yes, Theo, I can read the words on my little screen here. What's up?"

"My front tire has been slashed again. Flat as a pancake. It happened outside the VFW while I was meeting with the Major."

"Where are you?"

"On Bennington Street, near Fourteenth."

"Stay where you are. I'll be there in ten minutes."

Theo sat on a bus bench with his disabled bike nearby,

and thought about Brian and Edward. Both were nice kids from good families. Both had lockers very close to Theo's, and neither had a reason to slash his tires, throw rocks through his window, break into a computer store, or plant stolen loot in his locker. Theo considered both of them to be friends. He did not know the seventh graders as well, though every Scout in the troop got along just fine. The Major insisted on it. Sam's father was a doctor and his mother was a dentist. Theo could not imagine him behaving like a hoodlum. Bart was a straight A student and perhaps the nicest kid in the world. Of the five, the only real suspect could be Isaac Scheer, a quiet kid who seemed moody, often troubled, and who wore his hair a bit too long and listened to heavy metal. The Scheer family had issues. An older sister had been arrested for drugs. The father was usually unemployed and rumored to prefer living off his wife's income.

Most importantly, Isaac had an older brother in high school. Since the Boone detective team believed the attacks on Theo were the work of at least two people, Isaac and his brother fit in nicely. As always, though, when picking suspects, Theo was stopped cold by the question of motive. Why would Isaac and his brother, or anyone else for that matter, go to such trouble to ruin his life? It made no sense.

Mr. Boone arrived in his SUV. He opened the rear hatch, lifted Theo's bike, and shoved it inside, on top of his golf clubs. Judge, who had arrived riding shotgun, was demoted to the backseat. Theo sat in the front, arms crossed, eyes fixed straight ahead as they drove away. Nothing was said until Theo realized they were not headed in the direction of the Boone home. "Where are we going, Dad?" he asked.

"To the police station."

"Okay. Why?"

"Because I want the detectives to see firsthand what we've been telling them. Someone is stalking you and trying to frame you for a crime you did not commit."

Theo liked the idea. They parked on the street next to the police station. "Wait here," Mr. Boone said, and he slammed his door and marched into the building. Minutes passed as Theo talked to Judge and explained what was happening. Judge seemed to be confused. Detective Vorman appeared with Mr. Boone, who popped the hatch and slid the bike onto the rear bumper. Theo got out of the SUV and walked around to join the conversation.

"Look at this," Mr. Boone said firmly as he lifted the front tire and pointed to the hole in the sidewall. "This is the third one this week."

Vorman looked closer, touched the tire, and said, "It's definitely a deliberate puncture."

"It certainly is," Mr. Boone replied.

"And where did this happen?" Vorman asked.

"Outside the VFW, same place the rear tire was punctured last Tuesday," Theo said.

"What am I supposed to do with this?" Vorman asked.

Mr. Boone shoved the bike back into the SUV and slammed the hatch. "You're supposed to realize that whoever is slashing these bike tires and throwing rocks through our office windows is the same person who is trying to frame my son for the burglary. That's what you're supposed to do with this. You're supposed to realize you're wasting your time investigating, and accusing, Theo of a crime."

Go get him, Dad, Theo almost said.

"How can you be so sure these crimes are related?" Vorman asked with his usual sneer.

"I guarantee you they're related, and until you understand that they are, you're not going to figure out who broke into the computer store. While you waste your time, though, lay off my son. He's not guilty."

"Of course he's not, but you're the father, right?" Vorman said, his voice rising, his irritation apparent. "I wish I had a dollar for every mother and father who've sworn to me that their precious loved ones were innocent. We'll handle the investigation, Mr. Boone, with no help from you. And, as of now, and until we find something to the contrary, your son is still the leading suspect. All evidence points to him." Vorman pointed an angry finger at Theo, then turned and walked away.

Theo felt worse as they drove away, and he assumed his father did, too. Gil's Wheels was closed, so they headed home.

"Are you playing golf tomorrow?" Mr. Boone asked.

"Sure," Theo said with no enthusiasm.

"It's supposed to rain."

"I'm sure it will." Why not end a bad week with a heavy rain and a washed-out golf game?

Friday dinner was usually a trip to Malouf's, a Lebanese restaurant with great seafood, but neither Theo nor his parents were in the mood. They were tired from a long and quite unusual week. The constant anxiety was taking a toll on their moods. For three days now, Theo had thought of little else but being falsely accused, and arrested, and maybe sent to a prison facility for kids. He knew his parents were far more worried than they appeared. The latest tire slashing had rattled their nerves even more.

After a sandwich and a bowl of soup, Theo excused himself and went to his room. Ike had texted him three times during the afternoon, wanting to know if Theo had obtained the password to the law firm's digital file storage system. Theo had not answered the texts because he could not force himself to violate the firm's unwritten rules. Lifting the password from Vince's computer was a dishonest act, one that weighed heavy on Theo. Giving the password to Ike would only make the guilt worse. On the other hand, though, Theo was tired of running and tired of being the target of someone's carefully plotted conspiracy. It was time to fight back. The police seemed determined to nail him. The clock was ticking; time was against him. Before long the situation could get worse.

He called Ike, who was still at the office.

"It's about time," Ike said, irritated. "Did you get the password?"

"Yes, I did, but you gotta convince me, Ike, that this is the right thing to do."

"I've already told you that, Theo. We're not breaking any laws here. We're just snooping, that's all. Look at it this way, Theo. You can walk through the offices of Boone & Boone and see files everywhere, right?"

"Right."

"It's a law office. There are files on desks, files stacked neatly in cabinets, files left behind in the conference room, files in open briefcases, piles of files waiting to be stored away. Files, files, everywhere files. Now, Theo, have you ever picked up one of these files and flipped through it?"

A slight hesitation, then Theo said, "Yes."

"Of course you have, and you didn't break any law. You didn't violate any ethical rule because you're not yet a lawyer. You were just being nosy, that's all. Just snooping a little. That's all we're doing here, Theo, snooping. Some of the law firm's files are now stored in a digital vault, available to members of the firm for easier access. These same files exist in hard folders throughout the firm, the same kind of file you've peeked at before."

"I understand that, Ike, but it just doesn't seem right."

Ike breathed heavily into the phone, and Theo braced for a sharp rebuke. Instead, Ike calmly said, "I'm trying to help you here, Theo. Look at it like this. The information we're after will be kept between the two of us. We're not going to share client secrets with anyone. The privacy of the clients will not be violated in any way. We're just trying to solve a mystery, and if we're able to do so, no one will ever know that we've been snooping."

"But if you access the digital vault there will be a record of your entry."

"Don't worry about that, Theo. I'll use an encrypted code that cannot be traced. I'm a step ahead of you on this. I'm not your typical low-tech geezer, Theo."

"I didn't say you were."

"And, I'll bet the entry log is checked about once a year, right?"

"Probably."

"Give me the password, Theo."

"It's Avalanche88TeeBone33."

"Spell it."

Theo slowly spelled it, then gave him the account code.

"Smart move, Theo. I'll get to work."

Theo stretched out on his bed and stared at the ceiling. Ike was a smart man who'd once been a brilliant lawyer, but he often had strange ideas. His theory that Theo's problems were being caused by one of his mother's nasty divorces was pretty far-fetched. But, at least he had a theory. Theo was dwelling on Isaac Scheer, and the more he thought about him the less he was convinced the kid could be a real suspect.

Theo texted Griff: *Any luck finding the name of the guy selling 0-4s?*

He waited for ten minutes, then turned off his phone.

Chapter 19

Saturday morning, Theo awoke to the sounds of heavy thunder and raindrops pecking at his window. He slowly crawled out of bed and peeked through the curtains. Water was standing in puddles in the backyard. No golf today. Judge followed him downstairs where his parents were busy in the kitchen cooking pancakes and sausage and talking, of course, about the weather. Theo would never understand why adults spent so much time on the subject of the weather. They couldn't change it.

The town was buzzing with the news that Pete Duffy had been spotted at O'Hare International Airport in Chicago. He had tried to pay cash for a one-way ticket on a flight to Mexico City, but was delayed when the clerk noticed something odd about his fake passport. The clerk notified her supervisor. At that point, Duffy fled the ticket counter and disappeared into a crowd. The FBI identified him by lifting a fingerprint from the passport, and by analyzing video footage. There was a photo of Duffy on the front page of the Strattenburg newspaper, and he was not recognizable, at least in Theo's opinion. He was wearing some type of beret, thick-framed eyeglasses, the makings of a beard, and his hair was blond, almost white.

"The FBI has this technology that can enhance a photo of a person's face and see things not visible to the naked eye," Mr. Boone was explaining as if he knew a great deal about FBI techniques. Theo was at the table, eating pancakes, feeding some to Judge, staring at the black-and-white photo of Pete Duffy, and giving thanks that the man was back in the news. Maybe the town would spend a few days rekindling its interest in Pete Duffy and forget about that other criminal—Theo Boone.

"I wonder where he's been all week?" Mrs. Boone asked as she sipped her coffee and read the obituaries.

"Working on his new look, I guess," replied Mr. Boone. "Doing his hair, grooming his beard. A beret? Give me a break. A guy walking through O'Hare wearing a beret is bound to attract attention."

"It sure doesn't look like Pete Duffy," Theo said.

"It's him," Mr. Boone said with certainty. "He's changed

his looks, got some cash, bought him some new papers, though they must not be very good, and he almost got away."

"I'd like to get away," Theo said.

"Theo," Mrs. Boone said.

"It's true, Mom. I'd like to bolt out of here and go hide someplace."

"Things are gonna be okay, Theo," Mr. Boone said.

"Oh really? How do you figure that? I have the cops breathing down my neck, ready to haul me into Youth Court. And I have some crazy stalker chasing me all over town with a knife, ready to slash my tires again. Sure, Dad, things are really looking great."

"Relax, Theo. You're innocent and you will be proven innocent."

"Okay, Dad, here's the question. Do you think the person who robbed Big Mac's is the same person who's slashing tires, throwing rocks, and spreading all the garbage on the Internet?"

Mr. Boone chewed on a bite of sausage for a few seconds, then said, "I do."

"Mom?"

"I believe so."

"That makes three of us. To me it's pretty obvious. So why can't we convince the police of this?"

"I think we can, Theo," Mr. Boone said. "They're still investigating the break-in and burglary. I trust the police and I think they'll catch the criminals."

"Well, I think they've already decided it's me. That guy Vorman thinks I'm lying. I don't like him. He gives me the creeps."

"Things will be fine, Theo," Mrs. Boone said, patting his arm, then Theo saw her glance at his father. They held each other's gaze for a second or so, and it was not a look of confidence. They were as worried as Theo, maybe more. After breakfast, Theo and his dad drove to Gil's Wheels for yet another new tire. At Mr. Boone's request, Gil disappeared into the rear of his store and found the first two damaged tires. He gave them to Mr. Boone, who now had a collection of three. Mr. Boone paid for numbers two and three, and paid the eight dollars Theo owed on the first tire. Gil assured them that there was no epidemic of tire slashings in town; in fact, he had seen only three the entire week, all of which belonged to Theo.

Outside the bike shop, the rain had stopped, but the skies were still cloudy and threatening. For a moment, Theo and his father talked about driving to the golf course and waiting on the weather. The course, though, would be soaked, and if it was opened later in the morning there would be a crowd. Theo knew that a crowded golf course was worse than no course at all. They agreed that it was not a good idea.

Ike had texted twice during the morning and wanted to meet. Back home Theo puttered around the house and watched the weather. After an hour he announced that he was bored and explained to his parents that Ike had invited him for lunch. They said yes, and Theo took off on his bike.

Ike looked worse than usual. His eyes were red and puffy with dark circles just below them. "I've been up all night," he said as Theo took a chair. "Didn't sleep a wink. Spent the whole night reading through divorce files, and you want to know something, Theo, there are a lot of sad folks out there who need to get divorced. I've never been so depressed in my life. I don't know how your mother does this kind of work every day of the week. Wives accuse husbands of all manner of terrible behavior. Husbands accuse wives of even worse. They claw each other's eyes out over who gets the house, the cars, the bank accounts, the furniture, but man, when it comes to who gets the kids—it's worse than cage fighting. Horrible stuff, Theo."

Theo just sat and listened. Ike was hyper, probably jazzed on coffee and one of his little super juice drinks that guaranteed quick energy. He blitzed on: "So, I still like my theory. Do you?"

"Sure, Ike. It's the best theory yet."

"Thank you."

"They slashed my bike tire again yesterday, at the VFW."

Ike paused, pondered this, took a swig of coffee. "We gotta catch 'em, Theo."

"The police do not believe me, Ike."

"We gotta move fast." Ike picked up his notepad and flipped some pages. "I found two cases that we should explore. Both are nasty divorces from the Secured Docket, which, of course, means that the court has locked away the files, so only the lawyers have access. The first case involves Mr. and Mrs. Rockworth. I won't bore you with the details, but it's safe to say that Mr. Rockworth does not like your mother. Two children involved, huge fight over who should get custody, with both parents doing a pretty good job of proving that neither was fit to raise kids. After a bitter trial, Mrs. Rockworth was given custody and Mr. Rockworth was given liberal visitation rights with the kids, both of whom are in counseling. The judge ordered Mr. Rockworth to pay eighteen thousand dollars in attorney fees to the firm of Boone & Boone. Do you know anybody named Rockworth?"

"No. How old are the kids?"

"The boy is twelve, in the seventh grade at the middle school. He has an older sister who's fifteen. Evidently, both wanted to live with their father. The family has lived here for just a couple of years, which explains why you haven't heard of them."

"Is this your top suspect?"

"Oh no, just a possibility. I have a much better prospect—the fighting Finns! The divorce is far from final with a trial set for next month. These people have spent every dime they had trying to prove the other is a bigger creep. Mrs. Finn is pretty crazy and has done time in the nuthouse. Mr. Finn can't stay sober and tends to gamble too much. All kind of bad habits, on both ends. Three children, but the eighteen-year-old daughter has already left home. The other two are twelve and fourteen, both boys, and they really don't like their mother, who, of course, is represented by your mother. Tons of bad blood here, Theo, and it's safe to say that Mr. Finn and the two boys have an intense dislike for your mother and anybody else named Boone. This divorce has been going on for over a year and it's vicious. These people have driven themselves loony."

"What are the boys' names?"

"Jonah Finn, age twelve, seventh grade. Jessie Finn, age fourteen, ninth grade."

Theo closed his eyes and tried to place the names with faces, but he could not. "Don't know them."

"I thought you were a fairly popular kid at school, Theo. Do you know anyone?"

"I'm in the eighth grade, Ike. We don't mix too much with the seventh grade, nor does the seventh grade mix with the sixth, and so on. We have different classes, different schedules. How much do you know about these guys?"

"The basics, but not much more, at least for the younger one, Jonah. The court has appointed a guardian to look out for their best interests, and both boys have expressed a strong desire to live with their father. Their mother, through her talented lawyer, claims the boys want to live with their father because he lets them do whatever they want, including smoking cigarettes and drinking beer. Can you imagine a seventh grader drinking beer around the house with his dad?"

"No, I cannot. These are probably pretty tough kids, right?"

"They've had a rough life, moved around a lot, changed homes and schools. Not much stability. Yes, I'd guess that these two boys are pretty much on their own. Last year Jessie was caught with marijuana and went through Youth Court. He got probation. The boys were sent to a foster home three months ago as sort of a safe house, until the divorce was over, but they kept running away. As of now they're living with their mother, who works a night shift at the hospital. I doubt if there's much supervision. It's a mess, Theo, but these two boys are our prime suspects. Everything fits. A two-man team. A strong dislike for your mother. The motive to take revenge against you. The capacity to engage in vandalism and even burglarize a computer store. We need to find out more about them."

"I don't suppose my mother is involved in a divorce for a Mr. and Mrs. Scheer?"

Ike looked at his notes, flipped a page, then said, "No. Why?"

"Just a hunch. A kid I know in Scouts who's a little different, that's all."

"There's no file on them."

There was a long pause as Theo and Ike thought about the situation. Ike gulped coffee while Theo stared at the floor. Finally, Theo said, "I need to tell you about my friend Griff." Theo told the story of Griff's sister, Amy, and her friend Benny, and his friend Gordy, and the episode in which Gordy was offered a new Linx 0-4 Tablet for fifty dollars by some unknown kid in the high school parking lot. Ike's red eyes lit up when he heard this.

"This could be huge, Theo," he said.

"What if it's Jessie Finn who's trying to sell the tablet?" Theo asked.

"You gotta make this happen, Theo."

"But how?"

"If we can get our hands on a stolen tablet, we take it straight to the police who'll check the registration number. If it came from Big Mac's, then they'll get off your back and go after these little Finn thugs."

From a rear pocket, Ike pulled out his wallet, opened it, and withdrew some cash. He counted out two twenty-dollar bills and a ten. "Here's fifty bucks. Stick it in your pocket. Go find Griff, tell him to talk to his sister. Make this happen, Theo."

Theo took the money and stuck it deep in his pocket. He sat down again and said, "But what if it doesn't work? What if this Gordy guy doesn't want to handle a stolen tablet, or what if the dude has already sold it to someone else?"

"We won't know until we try. Do it, Theo. Get it done. And in the meantime, find out all you can about Jonah and Jessie Finn."

"Thanks, Ike."

"And don't worry about the fact that I snooped through

your mother's files. If it is the Finns, and if we solve this little mystery, I'll talk to Marcella and Woods and take all the blame. Believe me, I've done much worse."

"Thanks, Ike."

"You've already said that. Now get out of here."

"What about lunch?"

"I'm not hungry. I'm sleepy. See you later."

Chapter 20

The showers had stopped, but the skies were still threatening. Theo raced across town to Levi Park, on a bluff above the Yancey River, on the eastern edge of Strattenburg. As he pedaled furiously he was hoping the rain had not canceled the Farmer's Market because he was curious about Lucy the llama. Had she attacked Buck Baloney again? Had she attacked his sidekick Frankie? Would he, Theo, be forced to make another appearance in Animal Court to once more save Miss Petunia's beloved pet?

The market was still open, with many of the vendors huddled under tent roofs as their customers roamed about with shopping bags and umbrellas. The ground was wet and sticky, everyone's shoes and boots had at least an inch of mud on the soles. Lucy was next to Miss Petunia's booth, soaking wet but not perturbed at all. She looked harmless as two small children stopped and gawked. Across the way, on the other side of the entrance, a tiny man in a brown uniform was eating popcorn and talking to a lady who sold corn dogs. Theo presumed he was Frankie. Buck was nowhere in sight.

Theo said hello to Miss Petunia, who was delighted to see her lawyer. She squeezed him and thanked him again for his incredible courtroom heroics, and she happily reported that so far that morning Lucy had behaved herself, as had the two security guards. No spitting, no chasing, nothing out of the ordinary. No complaints from anyone.

Next to her booth was one displaying goat cheese, the handiwork of May Finnemore, who was sitting in a folding chair, knitting, while her spider monkey, Frog, hung from a tent pole that supported the roof over the booth. Why a spider monkey was named Frog had never been adequately explained to Theo. He had asked April, and more than once, but her response had been, "It's just my mother, Theo." So much of what May Finnemore did made little sense to anyone. Theo avoided the woman when possible, but not today. May stood and gave Theo an awkward hug. She said, "April's here."

"Where?" Theo asked, delighted that he would see her. April despised the Farmer's Market and rarely sat with her mother as she peddled her dreadful cheese. Theo had tasted it a couple of times and felt like vomiting whenever he saw or smelled it.

"She went that way," Mrs. Finnemore said, pointing at a row of booths.

"Thanks," Theo said, and disappeared as quickly as possible. Keeping a sharp eye out for Buck Baloney, he walked past dozens of vendors, most of them in the process of repacking their unsold goods and closing shop. April was standing near a tiny booth where an old bearded man was at work sketching in pencil the portrait of a teenage girl who was seated on a small crate in front of him. For only ten dollars "Mr. Picasso" would do your portrait in less than ten minutes. He had half a dozen samples on display—Elvis, John Wayne, and others.

Theo stopped next to April and said, "Hi."

"Hello, Theo," she said with a smile, then she turned and drew close for a better look at his face. "I thought you had a busted lip."

"I did. The swelling's gone."

She was disappointed with his wound. "How was the suspension?"

"Overrated. Pretty boring, really. I actually missed school." They began to slowly walk away. "What are you doing here?" he asked.

"My mom begged me to come today. She said we might need an extra eyewitness in case Lucy started spitting at people. So far, she hasn't felt the urge. What are you doing here?"

"I came to check on Lucy, to see if I might be needed in Animal Court again. Can we talk, in secret?"

"Sure." April was a quiet girl who understood the importance of secrets. Her family life was a wreck, and she often confided in Theo, who always listened thoughtfully. Now, it was her turn to listen. They sat at a small table near an ice-cream vendor, and when Theo was certain no one else could hear, he told April everything.

The ice-cream vendor was closing his booth and needed their table. They began walking again, slowly ambling toward the front of the market. "This is awful, Theo," she said. "I can't believe the police are accusing you."

"I can't either, but I guess I look pretty guilty."

"What do your parents think?"

"They're worried, and I get the feeling they're doing a lot of talking when I'm not around. You know how parents are."

"Not really. You have normal parents, Theo. I do not."

Theo wasn't sure how to respond to this.

"And Ike thinks it could be related to a bad divorce?"

"Yes, that's his theory, and it's a pretty good one. Nothing else makes sense."

"I sort of know Jonah Finn."

"You do?"

"Not well, just a little."

"What's the scouting report?"

She thought about this as they walked, then said, "Trouble, a loner, misfit, really smart guy who makes bad grades. I think his family is about as whacked-out as mine."

"How do you know this?"

"There's a guy in his class, Rodney Tapscott, who lives across the street from me, and he and Jonah hang out some. Do you know Rodney?"

"I know who he is, but I don't really know him. Doesn't he play the drums?"

"He tries to. We can hear him across the street."

"Can you talk to him?"

"About what?"

"About Jonah Finn. I need to find out all I can about this kid. Right now he's my only suspect and I need information."

"I'll see what I can do."

"And April, this is top secret. I can't get caught snooping around, and we can't accuse anybody of anything. This is a long shot, you understand?"

"Got it, Theo."

Other than April, the two friends Theo believed he could trust the most were Woody Lambert and Chase Whipple. Claiming the three needed to use a rainy Saturday afternoon to begin work on an upcoming project in Chemistry, Theo convinced his two friends to meet and make plans.

The truth was that Chase was the last person in the world Theo would partner with in a Chemistry lab. Chase was a brilliant, mad scientist with a long record of experiments gone haywire. He had started fires and set off explosions, and no lab was safe when Chase was at work. He had been banned from the labs at school unless a teacher was nearby for close surveillance. Woody was indifferent to Math and Science, but did well in History and Government.

They met in the basement game room of the Whipple home, and, after half an hour of Ping-Pong, they got down to business. Of course, first they had to replay the fight. Chase, who had never struck another person in anger, had witnessed the entire brawl and had been thrilled with the excitement. Woody reported that his mother yelled at him, then started crying. His father just shrugged and said, "Boys will be boys."

Theo swore them to secrecy. He even made them raise their right hands and promise to tell nothing, and when he was satisfied they could be trusted, he told them the entire story. Everything. The slashed tires, broken window, vandalized locker, planted loot, meetings with the detectives, everything. Then he got around to Ike and his research, though Theo did not confess to lifting the password from Vince's computer. He described how Ike had gone through the law firm's divorce files and identified a probable suspect, or suspects.

"That's brilliant," Woody said.

"It makes sense," Chase added. "The guy behind all of this is somebody who hates you and you don't even realize it."

Theo agreed, and then talked about the Finn boys and their parents' ugly divorce.

"My brother is in the tenth grade," Woody said. "I wonder if he knows Jessie Finn."

"We gotta find out," Theo said. "That's our project right now—to find out all we can about these two guys." Chase left to go upstairs and get his laptop. Woody pulled out his cell phone and called his brother, Tony, but got voice mail.

Theo called Griff who reported he had made no progress in getting the name of the ninth grader who was trying to sell black market 0-4 Tablets for fifty dollars. Griff promised to keep trying.

Mrs. Whipple, who was also a lawyer and close friend of Mrs. Boone, brought down a platter of cookies and a carton of milk. She asked how the Chemistry project was going and all three claimed to be excited with their progress. After she left, Chase went to the website of Strattenburg High School, and after a few minutes of browsing said, "There are three hundred and twenty ninth graders at SHS. Guess how many are named Jessie?"

"Four," Woody said.

"Three," Theo said.

"Two," Chase answered. "Jessie Finn and Jessie Neumeyer. We need to get the name from Griff."

"I'm trying," Theo said.

"Griff," Woody hissed. "I'm going to punch that kid out next time I catch him off campus. I can't believe he jumped on me like that. What a little twerp."

"Knock it off," Theo said. "As of now Griff is on our side. Besides, he apologized. So did Baxter."

"Baxter hasn't apologized to me. I'd like to see his eye right now. Probably black-and-blue."

Chase went to Google Earth and typed in the Finn's

address on Edgecomb Street, near the college. He zoomed in and said, "Here's their house." Theo and Woody huddled behind Chase, and all three looked at the screen. The Finn home was a two-story white frame on a street lined with several just like it. There was nothing different or remarkable about it. In the backyard there was a small, aboveground pool, and along the back fence there was a storage shed. The information was nice to have, but of no real value.

Theo's cell phone vibrated in his pocket. He yanked it out, opened it, looked at the screen, and said, "It's Griff."

Griff told Theo that his sister had finally made contact with Benny, and Benny had called Gordy, and Gordy had reluctantly said that the guy peddling the 0-4 Tablets was named Jessie somebody, didn't know his last name and really didn't know much about him. Griff assured Theo that his sister had not revealed the reason for her interest. Theo again stressed the need for secrecy.

"Now we're getting somewhere," Woody said.

"Why don't we go to the police?" Chase asked. "They can talk to both Jessies in the ninth grade and find out which one is trying to sell the stuff."

"It's too early," Theo said. "Suppose it's Jessie Finn. When the cops approach him, what's he gonna do? Admit he's got a stash of stolen computers and cell phones? Fall on his knees and confess everything? No way. He'll just deny it all, and if the cops can't find any of the loot in his backpack, they can't do anything. He'll get scared and we'll never find the stuff."

"Theo's right," Woody added. "We have to buy it from him. Then we give it to the police and they check the registration numbers."

"How are we going to buy it?" Chase asked.

"That's the big question," Theo said. "First, we start with Gordy. If he'll agree to help us, then he can hook up with Jessie Finn and buy the tablet."

"I don't know this Gordy guy," Woody said, "but I doubt if he's that stupid. Why would anyone get involved in this mess? We can't really expect him to buy a tablet he knows is stolen, and then hand it over to us when we're taking it straight to the police."

"He won't get into trouble," Theo said. "Not if he's helping solve a crime."

"I don't think so," Woody said.

"I agree with Woody," Chase said.

"What about Tony, your brother?" Theo asked.

"Are you sure he won't get into trouble?"

"I'm positive. If he helps the police find stolen goods, they'll thank him and pat him on the back. I happen to know the law, remember?"

"How could we ever forget," Chase said.

"Well, as you know, Tony will do anything. He's an idiot and loves to meddle in everybody else's business. That's a great idea, Theo. But where do we get fifty bucks?"

"I've already got it," Theo said.

Woody looked at Chase, who said, "Why am I not surprised?"

"Call him again," Theo said, and Woody pulled out his cell phone. He smiled as it was ringing, then said, "Hey, Tony, it's me." They talked for a few minutes and Woody did not mention their idea of getting Tony involved. Woody explained that they needed some inside dirt on a ninth grader named Jessie Finn. Tony did not know him but said he would start digging.

For half an hour, the gang of three kicked around ideas of how to nail the Finn boys, who by now were guilty beyond any doubt. Chase found their photos from a student directory and printed enlarged copies of their faces. Theo stared at the two, certain he had never seen them before. Jessie Finn had a Facebook page (Jonah did not), and Chase scanned it but found nothing that would interest them or help in their search for clues. Woody, who was sprawled on the sofa playing catch with a Ping-Pong ball, remembered a story. "You know, this makes perfect sense. I have two cousins who live near Baltimore, and last year their parents went through a nasty divorce. It was awful. I remember my two cousins saying bad things about their father's divorce lawyer. They really hated the guy, and I guess he was just doing his job. Does your mother worry about such things, Theo?"

"I'm sure she does, but she never talks about it."

"It's her job," Chase observed. The son of a lawyer.

Chapter 21

S unday morning, Theo sat in church between his parents and tried to listen to the sermon being delivered
by the Reverend Judd Koker, but it was a challenge.
In a cruel twist, the message was on the evils of thievery,
of stealing, and Theo felt as though he might be the target.
He had caught a few stares before the service began, and
almost bolted from the sanctuary when Mrs. Phyllis Thornberry happened by their pew and let it slip that they were
" . . . praying for Theo." Mrs. Thornberry was an ancient
member of the church and a terrible gossip, and Theo's parents somehow resisted the urge to inform her that Theo was
fine. Save your prayers for those who are truly in need.

Theo liked Reverend Koker because he was young and

energetic, and his sermons were sprinkled with humor and mercifully short. The old dude before him, "Pastor Pat" as he was known, had led the church for thirty years and was an awful preacher, in Theo's opinion. His sermons were long and dull and could force even the most devout worshipper into a near-comalike trance in a matter of minutes. Koker, though, knew the art of the short sermon, and so far in his brief ministry at the church, he had been well received.

The point of his sermon was that there are various ways in which we steal, and all of them are wrong in God's eyes. The Eighth Commandment proclaimed by Moses was Thou Shall Not Steal, which, of course, means it is wrong to take something that belongs to another person. Koker was expanding on this, though, to include other forms of theft. Stealing time away from God, family, friends. Stealing the gift of good health by pursing bad habits. Stealing from the future by missing opportunities in the present. And so on. It was pretty confusing. Theo glazed over fairly quickly and began thinking about the Finn boys, and, specifically, how he and his little gang might get their hands on some of the stolen goods the Finns were perhaps trying to sell.

Theo knew quite well that the first thing his father would say when they were in the car was, "Theo, how did you like the sermon?" For that reason, and none other, Theo tried desperately to pay attention.

Theo glanced around and realized he wasn't the only one drifting away. It was not a good sermon. His mind began to wander again. He asked himself how all of these fine people seated around him would react if "cute little Teddy Boone" got arrested and hauled into court. And what would they think if he couldn't come to church anymore because he was locked away in a juvenile detention center?

It was too awful to think about. Theo again tried to concentrate on the sermon, but his mind was racing. He began to fidget, and his mother squeezed his knee. He looked at his watch, but it seemed to have stopped cold.

It was the second Sunday of the month, and this caused an unpleasant mood in the Boone family. Second Sunday meant that Theo and his parents would not leave church and go directly home, where they would lunch on sandwiches, read the Sunday newspapers, watch a game on television, take naps, and in general observe a day of rest. No, sir. Second Sunday had evolved into a ritual so dreadful that Theo and his parents were having sharp words. The Boones and three other families had established a tradition of rotating brunch on the second Sunday of each month, which meant that Theo would be required to suffer through a long meal at a long table with a bunch of adults and listen to them talk about things in which he had little interest. Theo was a late child, and this meant that he was by far the youngest person invited to Second Sunday.

The oldest person was a retired judge named Kermit Lusk, who was also an elder in their church and a man of great wisdom and humor. He was pushing eighty, as was his wife, and their children were long gone. The rotation had brought the brunch to the Lusk home, a cramped and cluttered old house in bad need of a good sandblasting, at least in Theo's opinion. His opinions, though, were not worth much during these insufferable meals.

In the car, Mr. Boone said as he did every Sunday, "So, Theo, how did you like the sermon?"

"It was boring and you know it," Theo shot back, already mad again. "I fell asleep twice."

"It was not one of his better efforts," Mrs. Boone agreed.

They rode in silence to the Lusk home, the tension rising the closer they got. When they parked at the curb, Theo said, "I'll just stay in the car. I'm not hungry."

"Let's go, Theo," his father said sternly. Theo slammed the door and followed his parents inside. He hated these brunches and his parents knew it. Fortunately, Theo could sense some weakness on the part of his mother, perhaps a twinge of sympathy. She knew how miserable he was, and she understood why.

Inside, Theo managed a fake, metallic smile as he said
hello to Mr. and Mrs. Garbowski, a pleasant couple about the
same age as Theo's parents whose sixteen-year-old son, Phil,
threatened to run away from home if his parents forced him
to go to brunch on Second Sundays. The Garbowskis caved
in and Phil was still at home. Theo admired him greatly and
was pondering the same strategy. He said hello to Mr. and
Mrs. Salmon. He owned a lumber company and she taught
at the college. They had three children, all older than Theo
and none present.

Just great, Theo mumbled to himself. Eight adults and me.

Since nothing can make one hungrier than sitting in
church and waiting for lunch, the group soon took their
seats around the dining-room table. Judge Lusk gave a
quick prayer of thanks, and a housekeeper appeared with
the first course, a salad. A dry salad, Theo noted. Dressing
wasn't expensive, was it? Where was the dressing? But he
dove in, starved.

"What did you think of the sermon?" Judge Lusk asked.
Since all four families attended the same church, the sermon
was usually analyzed first. Great, thought Theo. Bad enough
to suffer through it live and in color, now I get tortured
again. Regardless of how bad a sermon might have been,
no one, over brunch, ever suggested that it was anything

short of brilliant. Even Pastor Pat had received rave reviews, though there had been some remarks like, "Perhaps he could've shaved off fifteen minutes."

The second course was baked chicken and gravy, and it was delicious. Theo, using perfect table manners because his mother was always watching, dug in and ate like a refugee. In her old age, Mrs. Lusk had stopped cooking, and this had been well received. Her housekeeper was an excellent cook. The Garbowskis would host the next Second Sunday, then the Boones. Theo's mother made no pretense of preparing a fine meal and always had it catered by a Turkish woman who fixed amazing dishes.

Much to Theo's delight, the conversation turned to Pete Duffy and his adventures of the past week. This sparked lively comments around the table as everyone wanted to rush in with their opinions and reports of the latest rumors. The verdict was unanimous—everyone was convinced Duffy had murdered his wife—and his flight from justice was further proof of his guilt. Mr. Salmon claimed to know Pete well and was of the opinion that he had stashed away plenty of cash and would probably never be found. Judge Lusk disagreed and argued that Duffy's close call at the airport in Chicago was proof that he would make another mistake sooner or later.

Theo ate in silence and listened with interest. The conversation was usually about politics and what was happening in Washington, but this was far more interesting. Then he had a miserable thought. Would these people one day soon be talking about him? Had any of these people ever been charged with a crime? He had serious doubts about that. Were the Boones and their son already the topic of hushed conversations behind their backs?

He cleaned his plate and waited on dessert. What he was really waiting on was two o'clock, the magic moment when it was time to go.

Late Sunday afternoon, Theo rode his bike across town and met April at an ice-cream parlor near Stratten College. April got a frozen yogurt and Theo got his favorite—chocolate gelato covered in crushed Oreos, and they found a booth away from the other customers.

"I talked to Rodney Tapscott," she said in a low voice. "I went over to his house last night and watched television."

Theo took a large bite and said, "Okay, I'm listening."

"Well, without sounding suspicious, I managed to get around to Jonah Finn. Rodney knows that you and I are close friends, so I was careful not to seem too nosy. Rodney said that Jonah is a weird kid who's been acting even stranger since his parents are divorcing, says he's real moody, even angry. Jonah doesn't have many friends. He bums money off of Rodney and other kids to buy lunch. His grades are getting worse; the kid's a wreck. He said that one day they were talking and Jonah said something about how much he dislikes your mother. I asked why was that. Rodney said it's because their father blames your mother for most of their problems, said that she's trying to make Jonah and his brother live with their mother, and they really don't want to."

"I kinda figured that," Theo said, glancing around.

"He said Jonah's father says bad things about your mother. All the money's going for legal fees, and on top of that your mother is trying to get Jonah's father to pay too much in child support and alimony. Rodney asked me if you're a good guy, and, of course, I said yes."

"Thanks."

"Don't mention it. Here's the interesting part. Rodney's never seen Jonah with a cell phone. Seventh graders are not supposed to have them at school anyway, but last week, he thinks it was Thursday, while they were on lunch break, Jonah showed him a new Excell SmartPhone. He said his father bought it for him. Rodney thought it was odd because the guy never has a dime."

"The store was broken into Tuesday night," Theo said, ignoring his gelato.

"That's right. Do you know what was stolen?"

"Just what was in the newspaper. Some laptops, tablets, cell phones, and a few other items."

"Excell SmartPhones?"

"I have no idea. The police do not release that type of information."

"It gets better. On Friday, they were in the library and Jonah was studying in a cubicle, one of those on the second floor by the computer lab. He was at a desk, all hunched over, as if he was trying to hide whatever he was doing. Rodney saw him and was curious. He managed to ease behind him, and he saw Jonah playing a video game on an eight-inch screen tablet."

"The Linx 0-4 has an eight-inch screen."

"Exactly. And there's no way Jonah can afford one."

Theo took a small bite but could taste nothing. "We have to get that tablet. Somehow."

"Any ideas?"

"No, not right now. Do you think Rodney would help?"

"I doubt it. He's not the type of kid who'll rat out a friend. He likes Jonah, says he's strange and all, but he also feels sorry for the kid. I didn't seem too interested in all of this because I didn't want to appear too eager."

"This is good stuff, April."

"Can't you just go to the police and tell them?"

"Maybe, I don't know. Let me think about it."

They discussed various plans, none of which seemed to work. As they were leaving, Theo thanked her again. April said she would do anything to help, legal or otherwise.

Theo headed home, but suddenly changed direction and went to see Ike.

Chapter 22

Pursuant to instructions from Mrs. Gladwell, Theo arrived at her office at 8:15 sharp on Monday morning. He sat across from her desk as she flipped through a file. She had yet to smile, as if still ticked off about the fight. "How was your weekend?" she asked, without the slightest hint of real interest.

"Okay, I guess," Theo said. He was not there to talk about his weekend; they had other business. His weekend had been fairly lousy, and he now realized that his life would not return to normal until his good name was cleared. He was still the accused, which was a dark cloud hanging over his head.

"Let's change the entry code to your locker," she said.

This was why she wanted to meet early, before classes started. "Do you have a new code?"

"Yes, ma'am. It's 529937." (Lawyer.)

She wrote it down, then compared it to the other codes. "I guess this will work."

Theo cleared his throat and said, "Mrs. Gladwell, I would like to say again how sorry I am for what happened last Thursday, you know, the fight and all. I broke the rules and I apologize."

"I expect better behavior out of you, Theo. I'm really disappointed and I want you to avoid any more trouble."

"I will."

She closed the file and managed a slight smile. "Did you talk to the police over the weekend?" she asked.

"No, ma'am."

"Have they finished their investigation?"

"I don't think so. As far as I know, they haven't caught the right people."

"Do they still suspect you, Theo?"

"As of last Friday, I was their main suspect."

She shook her head in disbelief.

Theo thought about Ike's advice, readjusted himself in the chair, cleared his throat, emitted an "Uh," and gave the clear impression that what he was about to say was not easy. "Mrs. Gladwell, if you knew a student here, a seventh grader, had a cell phone on campus, what would you do?"

She leaned back in her chair and chewed the end of her pen. "Well, I would talk to his or her homeroom teacher, ask her to approach the student, and if he or she had a phone, then we would confiscate it. The normal punishment is a half-day suspension, in school. Why do you ask this, Theo?"

"Just curious."

"No, you're not just curious. You know a seventh grader who brings a cell phone to school, don't you, Theo?"

"Maybe."

She stared at him for a long time, then began to figure it out. "Could this cell phone be stolen?" she asked.

Theo nodded and said, "Could be. Not sure, but it could be."

"I see. And could this stolen phone be linked to the break-in at Big Mac's last week?"

Theo nodded slightly and said, "Could be. I don't know for sure, and I'm not accusing anyone of the theft."

"The break-in is one thing, Theo, and it's really none of my business. The police are in charge of that. But the possession of a cell phone by a seventh grader is a violation of the rules here, on my turf. Let's deal with that first."

Theo stared at her but said nothing.

Another long pause. Mrs. Gladwell waited, and waited. She finally looked at her watch and said, "Okay, if you want me to help you, give me the name. If not, it's Monday morning and I have a thousand things to do."

"I feel like a snitch," Theo said.

"First of all, Theo, he or she will never know you told me. Second, and much more important, you're the prime suspect in a crime that someone else committed. If I were you, I would do everything I could to find the real criminal. Now give me the name or go to homeroom."

Trying to appear reluctant, Theo said, "Jonah Finn."

Ike had said he had no choice but to deliver the criminal.

The 8:50 bell rang for first period, and Mr. Krauthammer dismissed his seventh-grade homeroom. As the boys were filing out of the room, he took a few steps toward the desks, placed his hands on the shoulder of Jonah Finn, and said, "Could I see you a minute?"

When the room was empty, Mr. Krauthammer closed the door, and said, "Did I see you with a cell phone in the hall about ten minutes ago?" He, in fact, did not, but this was part of the strategy.

"No," Jonah snapped. He took a step back and looked thoroughly guilty.

"What's in your pockets?" Mr. Krauthammer asked, stepping toward him.

Jonah reluctantly removed a cell phone and handed it over. A half-day suspension would not bother him. He had seen worse. Mr. Krauthammer looked at the phone, an Excell 7 SmartPhone, and said, "Very nice. Come with me."

After a brief meeting with Mrs. Gladwell, Jonah was taken to a small study room in the library where he would be confined for the next four hours, under the watchful eyes of Mrs. Dunleavy, the librarian. His books were placed on a study table as if he were expected to plow through some extra homework as part of his punishment. Instead, Jonah put his head on the table and promptly went to sleep.

Mrs. Gladwell called Detective Vorman and gave him the registration number of the cell phone.

At Strattenburg High School, second period ended at 10:30 and was followed by a twenty-minute break. Tony Lambert, Woody's brother, tracked Jessie Finn from a distance and watched as he left the main building and walked into the large open courtyard where many of the students killed time on break and during lunch. Jessie sat by himself at a picnic table and was about to check his cell phone when Tony came out of nowhere.

"Hey, man, I hear you got some 0-4 Tablets for a good price," Tony said, glancing around as if a drug deal was in process.

Jessie eyed him suspiciously and said, "Who are you?"

"Tony Lambert, tenth grade," he replied, shoving a hand forward. Jessie shook it reluctantly and asked, "Oh yeah, where did you hear that?"

"Word gets around. How much are you asking?"

"For what?"

"For an 0-4. I got fifty bucks."

"Who told you I was selling something?"

"Come on, Jessie, word gets around. I really want that tablet."

"I don't have anything, man. I've already sold it."

"Can you get another one?"

"Maybe, but the price has gone up. Seventy-five bucks."

"I can get seventy-five. When can you get the tablet?"

"Here, tomorrow. Same time, same place."

"You got it."

They shook hands and Tony left. He walked inside the main building and sent a text to Woody. No deal, maybe tomorrow.

Theo's Monday morning had been uneventful. During homeroom, Mr. Mount made a big deal out of welcoming him and Woody back to school, and there were some smart comments from his classmates. Most, though, seemed to be proud of their two buddies for not being afraid to take a stand. In first period Spanish, Madame Monique asked Theo how he was doing and seemed a little too concerned about him. He brushed it off and said everything was fine. In second period Geometry, Mrs. Garman acted as though nothing had happened, which suited Theo just fine. During the morning break, April informed Theo that Rodney had passed along the news that Jonah Finn had been in homeroom, but then disappeared. Rodney did not know where he was.

While Jonah was napping in the library study room, Detective Vorman arrived at the school and met with Mrs. Gladwell. The two of them casually walked to a row of seventh-grade lockers, not far from Theo's, and she punched in the code for Jonah's. Inside they found the usual assortment of textbooks, notebooks, supplies, and junk. Hidden in a three-ring binder were two brand-new Linx 0-4 Tablets. They took them back to her office where Detective Vorman, using rubber gloves, removed the back panels and wrote down the registration numbers. They then returned to Jonah's locker and carefully replaced the tablets in the three-ring binder.

Detective Vorman thanked Mrs. Gladwell, left the school, and went to his desk at the police station where he checked the registration numbers against the list from Big Mac's System. Not surprisingly, they matched. He reported his findings to Detective Hamilton, and they decided to get a search warrant for the Finn home. Vorman filled in the blanks of a standard affidavit, a sworn written statement, and set forth the details of what he had found. He also included a statement that the subject's brother, Jessie Finn, had "allegedly" attempted to sell a Linx 0-4 Tablet to a classmate the previous week. Once the affidavit was completed and signed by Detective Vorman, he prepared a two-page search warrant in which he described the area he wished to search—the Finn home and its outbuildings. With his paperwork done, he walked four blocks down Main Street to the courthouse and left the affidavit and search warrant with the secretary for Judge Daniel Showalter, Youth Court, Division 1. The secretary informed him that the judge was in the middle of a hearing, and it might be two hours before he could review the affidavit and search warrant.

Detective Vorman walked back to his office, confident he had solved another crime, though a rather small one. He would have preferred to spend his time chasing drug dealers and serious criminals.

Chapter 23

At 3:15 Monday afternoon, Detective Vorman arrived at the school and went to Mrs. Gladwell's office. He waited as she walked to a classroom on the second floor and pulled Jonah Finn out of last period study hall. Jonah, who had already endured a half-day suspension, mumbled, "What's the matter now?" as he followed her from the room.

"Just follow me," she said, and the two walked without a word back to her office. They waited in the reception area by Miss Gloria's desk as the last bell rang and the students rushed out of the building. During the chaos of dismissal, Jonah and Mrs. Gladwell stepped into her office and closed the door. Vorman stood, flashed a badge, and said, "Are you Jonah Finn?"

He replied, "Yes." He looked at Mrs. Gladwell for help.

"Have a seat," Vorman said. "I'd like to ask you some questions."

"Is something wrong?"

"Maybe."

Jonah sat down and put his backpack in his lap. He was obviously frightened and not sure what to do or say.

Vorman sat on the edge of the desk and looked down at Jonah. It was not a fair fight. A tough cop in a dark suit and a frightful scowl glaring down at a scared, skinny kid with bangs in his eyes. Vorman knew exactly where the conversation was going; Jonah wasn't so sure.

The detective began: "We're investigating a burglary that happened last week at a computer store downtown, Big Mac's Systems, and I just have a few routine questions. That's all."

Jonah took a deep breath, almost gasped, and dropped his head. He stared at the floor, his mouth open in shock. Vorman had never seen a guiltier face. "That cell phone you got busted with this morning, where did you get it?"

"Uh, I bought it."

Vorman opened his notepad, licked his pen, and asked, "Okay, who'd you buy it from?"

"Uh, some guy named Randy."

Vorman scribbled on his notepad and asked, "How much did you pay for it?"

"Uh, fifty dollars."

"The phone was stolen from Big Mac's. Did you know it was stolen when you bought it?"

"No, sir, I swear."

"What's Randy's last name?"

"Uh, I'm not sure."

"Do you know where he lives? Where I can find him and go talk to him?"

"No, sir."

"Okay, so this mysterious guy Randy just pops up and offers to sell you a brand-new SmartPhone for fifty bucks, one that's valued at three hundred, and you don't think it might be stolen?"

"No, sir."

"That's not too smart on your part, is it?"

"I guess not."

"Are you lying to me?"

"No, sir."

"If you lie to me, Jonah, things will only get much worse."

"I'm not lying."

"I think you are."

Jonah shook his head, his bangs flopping in his eyes.

Vorman had spent years questioning tough criminals, men who could tell great lies with sincere faces. This kid was nowhere close to being believable. "The thief, or thieves, who broke into Big Mac's also took some tablets and laptops. Did Randy offer to sell you a brand-new tablet or laptop?"

"No, sir."

"Have you ever seen a Linx 0-4 Tablet?"

Jonah shook his head, his eyes still watching the floor.

"You know the school has the right to inspect your backpack and your locker," Vorman said, moving in for the kill. "Do you understand that?"

"I guess."

"Good. Let's take a look inside your backpack."

"What are you looking for?" Jonah asked.

"More stolen goods." Vorman reached for the backpack. Jonah clutched it for a second, then let go. Vorman placed it on Mrs. Gladwell's desk and slowly unzipped it. He removed textbooks, notebooks, a video game magazine, and then a tablet. A Linx 0-4. He held it up, examined it, and said, "Jonah, you lied to me. Where did this come from?"

Jonah leaned forward and placed both elbows on both knees, his head hanging low.

Vorman pressed on: "Jonah where did you get this? Did your brother give it to you?"

No response.

"Okay, let's go have a look inside your locker."

At about the same time, a mile away at the high school, Detective Hamilton introduced himself to Jessie Finn. They were in the principal's office, a few minutes after the final bell. Jessie's backpack was on the desk, unopened.

"I'd like to ask you a few questions," Hamilton began with a friendly smile. The principal, Mr. Trussel, was sitting at his desk, watching.

"About what?" Jessie asked with a sneer. He had been through the Youth Court system once and didn't like cops, or judges, or even lawyers for that matter.

"Do you have a brother named Jonah?"

"That's an easy question."

"Then answer it."

"Yes."

"Thought so. We have Jonah in custody right now, caught him with a stolen Excell 7 SmartPhone and three Linx 0-4s, one in his backpack, the other two still in boxes in his locker. Any idea where he got them?"

Jessie flinched, though he tried to seem unmoved. The

color drained from his face and it was pale. He shook his head, no.

"Didn't think so," Hamilton said. "We checked the registration numbers and we know where they came from. Do you Jessie?"

"No."

"Well, Jessie, at this moment your little brother is one scared boy. He's talking, singing like a bird, and he says that breaking into Big Mac's was all your idea, says he didn't want to do it, but you pressured him because you needed some help in hauling away all of the laptops, cell phones, and tablets. What do you think about that, Jessie? He's not a very tough kid, is he? I mean, he's your brother and he began ratting on you before we could even put the handcuffs on him."

"Handcuffs?" Jessie said with a dry, husky voice, his face confused and scared.

"Yep, and I've got a pair for you, too. Just hang on. Your little brother says that you two broke into the store through a back window last Tuesday night and took about a dozen cell phones, six fifteen-inch laptops, and ten Linx 0-4 Tablets. Says you guys were in the store less than five minutes because you had scoped out the place and knew where things were, plus you knew how to dodge the security cameras. Any of this ring a bell, Jessie?"

"I don't know what you're talking about."

"Oh, I think you do. Can I look inside your backpack?"

"Go right ahead," Jessie said, and shoved it at him. Hamilton unzipped it and slowly removed books, notebooks, a water bottle, a couple of magazines, nothing that appeared to be stolen. Hamilton shrugged and stuffed all of it back into the backpack. "Let's go take a look at your locker."

"You can't do that," Jessie said.

"Oh really? Why not?"

"It's a violation of my privacy."

"Not so fast, Jessie," Mr. Trussel said as he lifted a piece of paper. "This is a locker rental agreement you signed for the academic year. We don't require our students to use a locker, but when they choose to do so, they must sign this agreement. This clearly states that you must submit to a search of your locker when asked to do so by the school or the police."

"Let's go," said Detective Hamilton.

Back at the middle school, Detective Vorman and Mrs. Gladwell returned to her office, along with Jonah, who looked as though he was ready to cry. On her desk were the same two tablets she and Vorman had taken from Jonah's locker earlier in the day.

Vorman said, "We have your brother in custody over at the high school, and he's saying it was your idea to plant the three Linx Tablets in the locker of Theodore Boone. He's saying you hacked into the school's files, got the entry number, and placed the tablets there last Wednesday morning in an effort to frame Theo for the crime. True or false?"

"Jessie said that?"

"Oh yes, and plenty more. Right now he's sitting in a small room at the high school, in handcuffs, telling the entire story. Pretty sad, if you ask me, to rat out your little brother like this, but that's what happens when you do stupid things with an accomplice."

"I don't believe it."

"I don't care what you believe, son. You're in more trouble than you can possibly imagine. You're looking at breaking and entering, felony theft, stalking, conspiracy, vandalism. Your brother even says you slashed Theo's bike tires and tossed the rock through his office window."

"No! He did that!" Jonah blurted, then caught himself. He held his breath as he stared at the detective, who just smiled. In the heat of the battle, the kid had made a crucial admission. Vorman looked at Mrs. Gladwell. Both smiled. The mystery had been solved.

———

Back at the high school, the contents of Jessie's locker were stacked neatly on the floor of the hallway. Detective Hamilton, wearing surgical gloves, gently removed the last items—two Linx 0-4 Tablets. "Gee, I wonder where these came from," he said with a smile. "Jonah said we would probably find them here. Let me guess, Jessie, you have no idea how these shiny new things made their way into your locker, right?"

Jessie said nothing.

They stepped into an empty classroom and Mr. Trussel closed the door. "Sit there," Hamilton barked at Jessie as he pointed to a desk. Jessie did as he was told. There was no fight left in him.

"What I want at this point," Hamilton said as he hovered over Jessie, as if he might begin slapping him at any second, "is the rest of the stolen goods. Where are they?"

"I don't know what you're talking about," Jessie said feebly. His hands were clenched together on the desk and he stared at them.

Hamilton reached into a pocket and pulled out some papers. "You're a real smart kid, aren't you, Jessie? So tell me, what is a search warrant?"

Jessie shook his head.

"You don't know? Maybe you're not that bright after all."

Jessie shook his head.

"A search warrant allows the police to go into your house and search every room, every drawer, cabinet, closet, box, bag, every pile of junk in the attic, and every piece of old furniture in the garage. It allows us to turn your house upside down looking for the rest of the stuff you and your little brother stole from Big Mac's." Hamilton dropped his search warrant on the desk and it landed on Jessie's arms. He made no effort to read it.

"Is your mother at home, Jessie?" Hamilton asked.

"She's asleep. She works the night shift at the hospital."

"Well, let's go wake her up."

Chapter 24

Linda Finn was sound asleep in her bedroom on the ground floor of her home at about 5:00 p.m. Monday afternoon when the doorbell rang and jarred her awake. She never got enough sleep. She worked from 8:00 p.m. to 8:00 a.m., four days a week and occasionally on weekends for extra money. Such a weird schedule disrupted normal sleep patterns and kept her tired. And often, when she should have been sleeping, she was wide awake worrying about her bruising divorce, her worthless husband and his hardnosed lawyer, and her two boys and the bad direction in which they seemed to be headed. Linda had plenty to worry about.

The doorbell would not stop ringing, so she pulled on

an old bathrobe and walked to the front door in her bare feet. She opened the door. Staring at her was Detective Vorman, with Jonah, and behind them were two police officers in full uniform. Beyond them, at the curb, were two police cars, with lights and all the usual decorative painting and decals. There was an unmarked car in the driveway. She put her hand over her mouth and almost fainted.

Then she managed to open the storm door and said, "What is it?!"

Vorman flashed his badge and said, "Detective Scott Vorman, Strattenburg Police. May I come in?"

"What is it, Jonah?" she asked, horrified.

Jonah looked at his shoes.

"We need to talk," Vorman said, opening the storm door wider. She backed away, clutching her bathrobe to make sure she was decent. Vorman followed Jonah inside and closed the door behind them. In the driveway, Detective Hamilton sat in his car with Jessie in the passenger's seat. "Are we going in?" Jessie asked.

"Maybe," Hamilton replied. The two uniformed officers loitered in the front yard, smoking cigarettes. Across the street, a few neighbors were on their porches, watching with curiosity.

Inside, Vorman found a seat in an old chair with holes

in the fabric. Linda and Jonah sat on a sofa with battered cushions. "I'll get to the point, Mrs. Finn. A computer store on Main Street was broken into last Tuesday night. The thieves took some laptops, cell phones, and tablets. About twenty thousand dollars worth of stuff. Our prime suspects are Jonah and Jessie."

She jerked around and glared at Jonah, who was still fascinated by his shoes.

Vorman went on: "We've searched their lockers and backpacks, and so far we've recovered five of the tablets and one cell phone. We suspect the rest of the stuff might be hidden somewhere in this house, so we have a search warrant, signed by a judge, that allows us to look everywhere."

"Everywhere?" Linda gasped, immediately thinking of the stacks of unwashed dishes in the kitchen sink, the piles of dirty laundry in the basement, the unmade beds, the undusted furniture and shelves, the filthy bathrooms, the litter in the hallway, the half-empty glasses and cups in the den, and all of this was only the downstairs. The upstairs, where the boys lived and she was afraid to go, looked worse than a landfill.

"That's right," Vorman said as he pulled out the search warrant and handed it to her. She just gawked at it and shook her head.

"Every room, every closet, every drawer," Vorman said, cranking up the pressure. Vorman knew no woman would want the police or anyone else poking through their house.

"Is this true, Jonah?" she asked, her eyes suddenly wet. Jonah refused to speak.

"Yes, it's true," Vorman said. "Jessie has pretty much confessed to everything, but he will not tell us where the rest of the stolen goods are. So, we have no choice but to take the house apart and see if the stuff is here."

"Is it here, Jonah?" she demanded. He glanced at her, another guilty look.

"At this point, it's important to cooperate," Vorman said helpfully. "The judge will take it into consideration."

"If it's here, tell them," she said angrily to Jonah. "There's no sense in making the police dig through our home."

After a long pause, Vorman said, "Look, I don't have all afternoon and all night. I'm going to call for some extra men and we'll start by digging through the boys' bedrooms."

"Tell me, Jonah!" Mrs. Finn growled.

Jonah crossed his arms, bit his bottom lip, and finally said, "In the crawl space above the garage."

Sitting in the unmarked car, Jessie watched with horror as the policemen walked out of the garage with armloads of laptops, tablets, and cell phones. "Well, well, I guess they found everything," Hamilton said. "Stay here." He got out of the car to go have a look. Jessie wiped a tear off his cheek.

Linda Finn quickly got dressed and followed the police downtown. Jessie was riding in the car in front of her. Jonah was with Detective Vorman in another car. She cried all the way, asking herself—How could this happen? What had she done wrong as a mother? What would they do with her boys? How would this affect her divorce and her battle to win custody of Jonah and Jessie? Would custody be an issue if they were sent away? A hundred questions raced through her mind as the little caravan moved through the streets of Strattenburg.

At the police station, they gathered in a small room in the basement, and for the first time since that morning Jonah and Jessie were face-to-face. Jessie looked as though he wanted to punch his little brother. Jonah was thinking what a rat his big brother was. But they could say nothing.

Detective Hamilton took charge by saying, "This crime has been solved and you boys are in some serious trouble, no sense in beating around the bush. You're not going home tonight, and you may not be home for quite a while."

Linda started crying again. After a few sobs, she managed to ask, "Where are you taking them?

"There's a juvenile detention center down the street. They will appear in Youth Court the day after tomorrow and the judge will decide what to do with them at that point. A formal hearing will be held in about a month. Any questions?"

A thousand questions, but none spoken.

Detective Hamilton said, "I'm going to ask Detective Vorman to explain your Miranda Rights. Listen carefully."

Vorman slid across two sheets of paper, one for each boy. "These are the same. Number one: You have the right to remain silent. Number two: Anything you say in this meeting may be used against you in court. Number three: You have the right to an attorney, and if you can't afford one, the court will provide you with one."

"Just like on television," Jessie said, the wise guy.

"You got it," Vorman said. "Any questions? Okay, sign those forms at the bottom. Mrs. Finn, as their mother, you sign just under their names."

The Finns reluctantly signed their names. Vorman collected the sheets of paper. Hamilton looked at Jonah and Jessie, and said, "I've been through this a thousand times, and I can promise you that the most important thing you can do right now to help yourselves is to cooperate. You're guilty. We know you're guilty. We can prove you're guilty. So none of this pointing fingers at everybody else. The judge, the same guy who decides if you're gonna be sent away to juvenile detention, and for how long, will ask me in court if you boys cooperated. If I say yes, he likes that. If I say no, then he frowns and doesn't like that. Understand?"

"I want a lawyer," Jessie said.

"We can sure get you one," Hamilton shot back. "Scott, take him to jail."

Vorman jumped to his feet, snapped a pair of handcuffs off his belt, grabbed Jessie by the neck, pulled him up, and cuffed his hands behind his back. He opened the door and was about to take him away when Linda slapped the table and said, "Wait a minute! I want the truth! I want you two boys to tell me the truth. Sit down, Jessie. Sit down right here and tell me what happened."

Vorman released Jessie, who was stunned at the speed with which he got himself handcuffed. Carefully, he sat on the edge of his chair, his hands still cuffed behind his back.

When everyone took a deep breath, Jonah said, "We did it because we needed the money."

Chapter 25

Theo was in the middle of his homework when his father's voice came across the office phone intercom. "Hey, Theo."

"Yes, sir."

"Could you please step into the conference room?"

"Sure."

Both parents were there, and his mother had been crying. "What's the matter?" Theo asked.

"We have some good news," his father said.

"Then why is Mom crying?"

"I'm not crying, Theo," she said. "Not now."

His father said, "I just talked to Detective Vorman. They've arrested two boys, brothers, Jonah and Jessie Finn, for the break-in at Big Mac's. The police found most of the stolen goods in the boys' home."

"Their mother is my client, Theo," Mrs. Boone said sadly.

No kidding, Theo thought, but said nothing.

Mr. Boone continued, "The boys have confessed to everything, including their little campaign of terror against you. Seems they were carrying a pretty substantial grudge because of the divorce."

"I'm so sorry, Theo," Mrs. Boone said. "I should have realized this."

Theo took a deep breath and smiled and thought about Ike. His crazy uncle had solved the mystery long before anyone else had a clue. "This is great," Theo said. "The flat tires, the rock, the Internet stuff, everything?"

"Everything," his father said. "The break came when someone at school reported that the younger boy, the seventh grader, had a cell phone in his pocket. As you know, that's against the rules, and the cell phone turned out to be one that was stolen from the store. One thing led to another, more stolen goods were found in the boys' lockers, and then the police got a search warrant."

Theo felt as though someone was reading secrets he'd written about himself. He managed to smile and nod happily along, and he wasn't really faking it. Theo was delighted this little nightmare was over. "What's gonna happen to them?" he asked.

"That will be determined in Youth Court," Mrs. Boone said. "The older one, Jessie, has a record and I suspect he'll be sent away. Jonah will probably get probation."

"What does this do to you and your client, their mother?" Theo asked.

"I can't represent her, Theo. I'll withdraw tomorrow as her lawyer. Her boys attacked you because of me, and I should have realized it. I'm so sorry."

"Please, Mom, you had no idea."

"It's the right thing to do, Theo," Mr. Boone added. "We may have to appear in Youth Court and talk about what these two guys did. Your mother cannot represent Mrs. Finn when we may have to testify against her sons. I know it's sticky, but there's no other choice."

Theo shrugged, secretly delighted that all Finns would be gone from Boone & Boone.

Theo was thrilled. His parents were relieved. Even Judge looked happier.

"It's Monday," Theo said. "I'm going to run over and see Ike."

Bob Dylan was playing softly on the stereo. Ike was smoking a pipe and a cloud of blue fog hung over the room. Theo had sent Ike a dozen text messages throughout the day to keep him posted. His last one read: *Finns arrested. Full confessions. Whoopee.*

"Congratulations, Ike," Theo said as he dropped the fifty dollars on Ike's insanely cluttered desk. "You did it."

Ike grinned because it was not the right moment for modesty. "What can I say? I'm a genius."

"Beautiful, Ike. Just beautiful."

"What kind of mood is Marcella in?"

"Not too good. She's blaming herself."

"She should have realized, Theo. Marcella is too smart not to have suspected something from one of her cases."

"Don't blame her, Ike. She feels lousy enough."

"Okay, but if I thought about it, then she should have thought about it, too."

"Agreed. Are we going to tell her about snooping through her files?"

Ike kicked back and put his feet onto his desk, knocking off a few files in the process. "You know, Theo, I've been thinking about that. Now is not the time to come clean."

"So when?"

"Don't know. Let some time pass. Everybody's kinda

edgy right now. Your parents have been worried sick. Let things cool down, and then we'll discuss the matter, just the two of us."

"I'd feel better if we told my parents everything."

"Maybe you would, maybe you wouldn't. Look, Theo, honesty is a great virtue. You should always strive to be honest and trustworthy, and if your mother asked you tonight if you stole the password, gave it to me, and thus allowed me access to her divorce files, you would say Yes. That would be the honest thing to do. Right?"

"Right."

"But she doesn't know, and she may never know. Therefore, is it dishonest not to tell her?"

"It feels dishonest."

"You're thirteen years old. Have you told your mother every bad thing you've gotten away with in your life?"

"No."

"Of course not. No one does, Theo. We all have our little secrets, and as long as they're harmless, who really cares? With time, the secrets often go away and things don't matter anymore."

"What if someone checks the entry record to the firm's InfoBrief and sees that it was accessed off-site?"

"Well, if you are confronted, then you tell the truth. And, I'll step in, tell the truth, too, and take all the blame."

"You can't take all the blame, Ike, because I stole the password."

"Under the circumstances, it was the right thing to do. I'll have a little chat with your parents and explain that I insisted on looking at the files. We'll fight and all that, but we've been fighting for a long time. Sometimes you gotta fight, Theo. Remember?"

"I guess, but I still don't feel good about it."

"Let's do this, Theo. Let's not mention this issue again for one full month. I'm writing this down. One month from today we'll discuss it again."

Theo thought about it for a moment, then reluctantly said, "Okay." Theo knew, though, that it was not okay, and he knew it would bug him until he told his mother everything.

"Mom says you're invited to dinner tonight at Robilio's."

"Tell her I said thanks."

"I need to go. I don't know what to say, Ike. You're the greatest."

"Not the greatest, Theo, but maybe in the top five."

Theo bounded down the steps, hopped on his bike, and headed for the office. He pedaled furiously as he flew down the street. Everything seemed lighter—the air, the mood, the bike.

Theodore Boone, no longer the accused.

Read where it all began . . .

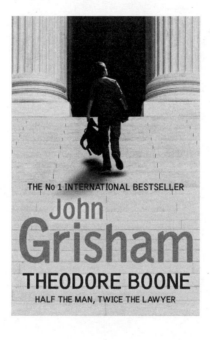

THE No 1 INTERNATIONAL BESTSELLER

John
Grisham

THEODORE BOONE

HALF THE MAN, TWICE THE LAWYER

HODDER &
STOUGHTON

Theodore Boone was an only child and for that reason usually had breakfast alone. His father, a busy lawyer, was in the habit of leaving early and meeting friends for coffee and gossip at the same downtown diner every morning at seven. Theo's mother, herself a busy lawyer, had been trying to lose ten pounds for at least the past ten years, and because of this she'd convinced herself that breakfast should be nothing more than coffee with the newspaper. So he ate by himself at the kitchen table, cold cereal and orange juice, with an eye on the clock. The Boone home had clocks everywhere, clear evidence of organized people.

Actually, he wasn't completely alone. Beside his chair, his dog ate, too. Judge was a thoroughly mixed mutt whose

age and breeding would always be a mystery. Theo had res-
cued him from near death with a last-second appearance in
Animal Court two years earlier, and Judge would always be
grateful. He preferred Cheerios, same as Theo, and they ate
together in silence every morning.

At 8:00 a.m., Theo rinsed their bowls in the sink, placed
the milk and juice back in the fridge, walked to the den, and
kissed his mother on the cheek. "Off to school," he said.

"Do you have lunch money?" she asked, the same
question five mornings a week.

"Always."

"And your homework is complete?"

"It's perfect, Mom."

"And I'll see you when?"

"I'll stop by the office after school." Theo stopped by the
office every day after school, without fail, but Mrs. Boone
always asked.

"Be careful," she said. "And remember to smile." The
braces on his teeth had now been in place for over two years
and Theo wanted desperately to get rid of them. In the
meantime, though, his mother continually reminded him
to smile and make the world a happier place.

"I'm smiling, Mom."

"Love you, Teddy."

"Love you back."

Theo, still smiling in spite of being called "Teddy," flung his backpack across his shoulders, scratched Judge on the head and said good-bye, then left through the kitchen door. He hopped on his bike and was soon speeding down Mallard Lane, a narrow leafy street in the oldest section of town. He waved at Mr. Nunnery, who was already on his porch and settled in for another long day of watching what little traffic found its way into their neighborhood, and he whisked by Mrs. Goodloe at the curb without speaking because she'd lost her hearing and most of her mind as well. He did smile at her, though, but she did not return the smile. Her teeth were somewhere in the house.

It was early spring and the air was crisp and cool. Theo pedaled quickly, the wind stinging his face. Homeroom was at eight forty and he had important matters before school. He cut through a side street, darted down an alley, dodged some traffic, and ran a stop sign. This was Theo's turf, the route he traveled every day. After four blocks the houses gave way to offices and shops and stores.

The county courthouse was the largest building in downtown Strattenburg (the post office was second, the library third). It sat majestically on the north side of Main Street, halfway between a bridge over the river and a park filled with gazebos and birdbaths and monuments to those killed in wars. Theo loved the courthouse, with its air of authority, and people hustling importantly about, and somber notices and schedules tacked to the bulletin boards. Most of all, Theo loved the courtrooms themselves. There were small ones where more private matters were handled without juries, then there was the main courtroom on the second floor where lawyers battled like gladiators and judges ruled like kings.

At the age of thirteen, Theo was still undecided about his future. One day he dreamed of being a famous trial lawyer, one who handled the biggest cases and never lost before juries. The next day he dreamed of being a great judge, noted for his wisdom and fairness. He went back and forth, changing his mind daily.

Do you wish this wasn't the end?

Join us at www.hodder.co.uk, or follow us on Twitter @hodderbooks to be a part of our community of people who love the very best in books and reading.

Whether you want to discover more about a book or an author, watch trailers and interviews, have the chance to win early limited editions, or simply browse our expert readers' selection of the very best books, we think you'll find what you're looking for.

And if you don't, that's the place to tell us what's missing.

We love what we do, and we'd love you to be part of it.

www.hodder.co.uk

 @hodderbooks

 HodderBooks

 HodderBooks